The House
on
Dundas and Vine

Published by Ricky Dale
Publishing partner: Paragon Publishing, Rothersthorpe
First published 2022

ISBN 978-1-78222-905-6

Book design, layout and production management by Into Print
www.intoprint.net
+44 (0)1604 832149

A story about love from the pen of

RICKY DALE

A semi-fictional story inasmuch as the stories within the story are true!

Thanks and Acknowledgments

The help that came from family and close friends during the writing
of *The House on Dundas and Vine* has been all-important to me.
I am indebted to:
Dr. Kimberley Jayne; Dianne Letky; Mark Kay; Pete Layland.

Especial thanks to my assistant Karoline Stanton and also to
Mark and Anne Webb of Paragon Publishing.
All of whom I had the good fortune to come across three
books ago, and without whom I would have struggled to bring
these novels to fruition.

Getting to know you
Extracts from a recorded conversation with the author:

I lived in British West Africa as a child. There were no schools and such in those days and so I amused myself composing reams of poetry. Oftentimes my somewhat precocious self would see me singing at one or another of Mom and Dad's adult soirées too.

When eventually the family moved to North America, it seemed to me a natural progression to involve myself in singing more seriously.

During those early years in North America, Britannia did not rule the music scene and so, to some extent, I was considered unique. It wasn't long before I was snapped up by the fabulous *Brant Inn* to become their in-house singer. I was fortunate to catch the tail-end of the pre-rock crooners, and even when that came to an end, as long as you were clean-cut and called 'Bobby' or 'Ricky', work was endless!

Things were going well for me until the arrival of all the 'mopheads' – you know, groups rather than singers. Although I still had a career for a while, it was in reduced circumstances. I found that in some clubs and bars I was earning less than when I first started.

For me the whole status of music per se had died. Although I was courted from time to time, I realised that essentially the moment had come to move on.

I seemed to be taken seriously in business, and so that's where I landed for the following decades, until retirement came knocking.

Poetry had remained my passion but the thought that rocked my boat was to attempt writing a full-blown novel. This novel is my 6th attempt to date – I really hope that you will enjoy it.

Ricky Dale, November 2021

The House on Dundas and Vine

"A very impressive literary achievement, so full of delights."
– Matiste Bernstein –

"Blood, sweat and tears are the lifeblood of Ricky's phraseology, inasmuch as he is able to take you where you haven't been a thousand times before."
– Susan Alexander (Eve) –

"A mesmerising read about somewhat ordinary people doing extraordinary things in a quite ordinary way!"
– Jerry Thompson –

" A touching book; and so funny, so likeable."
– Paul; screening room reporter –

"Warms the heart, amuses the mind and is unreservedly recommended."
– Leland Carter –

PREFACE

There is in all likelihood some truth and justification in the rumour that I have oftentimes sought to condemn 'so-called' romantic narrative as being 'written by morons'. Not necessarily as a result of the literacy of some, but conversely as the consequence of the subject matter.

Although it is not hardly proper or ethical to tar all with the same brush – perhaps enough to say that when attempting to scope-out love's complexities writers should 'savvy-up'!

It seems to me that true love ways are surely not a façade of inert gaucheness as is often portrayed.

Ricky Dale

When the first flake falls on Hamilton, Ontario, the whole city is given to pretending it's the first snowflake ever ...

FOREWORD

Just you know why
Why you and I
Will by and by
Know true love ways

Sometimes we'll sigh
Sometimes we'll cry
And you'll know why
Just you and I
Know true love ways

Throughout the days
Our true love ways
Will bring us joys to share
With those who really care

Sometimes we'll sigh
Sometimes we'll cry
And we'll know why
Just you and I
Know true love ways.

Acknowledgements to Charles Hardin Holley, otherwise known as the lamented genius – Buddy Holly

CONTENTS

The House on Dundas and Vine

I

Pi's story

"I have regrettably been asked to inform you that Ethan Edwards has been reported as missing. On behalf of the Secretary of Defense I extend my deepest sympathy."

It was late summer and right across the bushland the sun was shining like an instrument of torture – the type of day when you ought to count your blessings that you are home and out of it.

I often took in neighbours' clothes for ironing and had quite a large batch to finish – one posh lady even liked her panty-hose ironed! I didn't mind ironing at all – it was a task that I found rather pacifying at times.

There's not much I can say about the police officer who had knocked upon my door, nor the chaplain who was stood a few feet behind him. They were incapable of uttering a single word, as was I. I guess we knew that 'missing' was merely a euphemism for 'dead'. Be that as it may, I still needed to hear whether my dad was coming home or not – in clear plain language!

My dad was killed during the Battle of la Drang Valley. At that certain moment I reached a sort of impasse. I questioned it and it seemed that there weren't even any stars left in the sky, only some horrible iniquitous darkness left. Dad and I had planned so much and now something had chosen to set us apart from all that we had and all that we were gonna have. Miniscule by miniscule I thought the pain was going to consume me until there was Gloria and her House on Dundas and Vine!

Gloria had 'listenability' and I let the words flow:

"For heaven's sake my dad wasn't even ever supposed to be in Vietnam. He hadn't been called upon to enlist. I sometimes wondered whether he figured it all out mathematically! He told me that he had allegiance to both the United States and Australia and added "Australia is in the war in any event and I am also an Australian National Pi."

My dad was not a fighter by any stretch; he was a mathematician – the best! Dad didn't even condone fishing as a sport. "Everything is constructed of numbers" he said. That's why he came to nickname me 'Pi'.

With regard to my mom – she lived in a sort of oblivion to the real world. After she left with the guy who mowed our lawn, I remember the utter relief that came over me!

Dad's mom (my dear grandma Boo) had referred to what was ailing my mother as being what she called 'menstruation hysteria'. "Don't let you and dad be fazed by her bad attitude" she'd say. Then she would always finish off the sentence by briskly adding "stand tall our Pi, that's what our family always do."

Dear grandma, she meant well, but what she didn't at all realise was that mother's uncontrollable bursts of violence were only ever dealt out to my dad and me behind closed doors. To all and sundry butter wouldn't melt in mother's mouth.

After a while dad and I began corresponding with several ladies his similar age and status in the United States. I say 'dad and I' because I often typed the letters for dad; he was rubbish on a typewriter! Dad was quite optimistic regarding our new venture and so was I. He remarked that it could possibly be a new and exciting beginning for us both.

We received quite a bundle of really nice replies. Often letters were sent from a part of the United States that dad and I weren't familiar with and we would become excitable trying to locate them in our old school atlas.

More often than not the writers had enclosed a photograph of themselves and/or their family. I thought some of those American ladies looked like movie stars and was ever so excited by the prospect of having an American mom.

Terry the postman had been an old school buddy of dad's and we felt we had to be honest with him as to why there had suddenly become such a large influx of mail from the United States.

He sat on our steps one day with a pile of U.S. letters on his lap, called me over to him and said "Inside one of these envelopes may be your new mom Pi". He squeezed my hand and added "I really hope so!" It was true, dad and I were going to make it all happen, I just knew we were.

After just over a year it really did start to become a reality. We had sold our home and every stick of furniture. We were able to transport some of my old treasured toys, but most of the larger items, like the rocking horse and my doll's house etc, well we decided to sell them to give me some extra pocket money. Dad said that drawing the line about what to sell and what to keep was an all-important factor when moving to another country and I knew he was right.

My newly intended mom was called Chris. Dad and Chris had spent a whole bunch of money speaking on the telephone and I had spoken to Chris too. She sounded really nice. She had a son and daughter around my age and I had spoken to her daughter as well. Dad told me that Chris was a widowed lady whose husband had been a police officer.

Well eventually we set sail on the SS America and, before you knew it, we were all hugging at the docks. When I think about it now, it was fascinatingly awesome how we all gelled. We just didn't consider ourselves as strangers in any respect from that point on.

Chris, Megan and Paul lived in a small Georgia town called Cornelia. Their home was an old updated ranch-style house with an enormous wooded backyard. I remember thinking how stunningly American everything was – the American flag fluttering on the outside porch and especially the huge super 'eat-in' kitchen with a plethora of cooking paraphernalia hanging from the ceiling.

Before we had even started to unload our suitcases from the station wagon the very first Georgia snowflakes began to fall in a cornucopia of gay confusion. Chris smiled and drawled "We said a prayer last night for snow and it looks to me like it was answered – we had a hunch that you Australian folk would really appreciate some Georgia snow."

Although it was still only early December (1964) it felt like dad and I had spent all of our lives here. That elusive cosy new beginning had become ours. We were both home at last.

Chris had already made enquiries and quickly found me a place at Southern Polytechnic to commence after Christmas. Dad had easily got fixed up with a teaching position at Chattahoochee Technical Institute which was quite nearby too.

The days slipped away into the next and nearing the last. Dad said he couldn't remember us having such contentment without the contention. It was indeed a new experience for us both until our day stealthily came to an abrupt finish.

Christina's lawyers swung into action to have me legally adopted in order to avoid any potential immigration issues at a later date and, from the onset, Paul and Megan were always there to shore me up. I boundlessly adored my reborn family more than words could possibly describe and yet, just being in the same house with them without my dad being there as well, seemed meaningless. His absence was pure and unadulterated.

A home was not a home without him there.

It didn't take long for me to decide to fly the nest, perhaps to another town where dad being 'gone' was past.

My new family 'ganged up' on me in the nicest way possible. They didn't want me to go! However, after many attempts of persuasion we all finally reached what seemed like a very amicable agreement indeed; that I would go live with Christina's cousin Gloria in southern Ontario. Assuming that Gloria was minded to have me, Christina thought that the new location was far enough away to give me a more positive perspective.

Christina wrote to Gloria that same evening and astonishingly enough we received a reply within just several days which must have been by return. It confirmed "your young lady, or should I say 'your daughter' would be welcome to be my companion at 'The House on Dundas and Vine'. In fact I would be quite reconciled to have her here" – quite reconciled??

Chris said that Gloria was the only female streetcar driver 'between hell and kingdom come' which was how her co-workers had branded her. She was prim, fussy and didn't cotton to folks who cussed. She said I should mind my p's and q's and, if I did, I would fit in real fine!

It may well be the first time that crystal ever pierced the steel –
(an apology to Joan Baez)

2

Ricky's story

Gloria was a streetcar driver and I loved her. In those days I sang at a club downtown and each evening after my singing was done she always drove the last bus home. I would often sit by the window just so as I could see her in the reflection.

I don't know what first drew me to her – perhaps it was those sad dark eyes beneath the tinted bifocals she wore? It wasn't at all like I made a habit of falling in love with total strangers – withal at work I saw dozens of pretty girls who I never wanted to know – perhaps it was Gloria's yellow hair too!

I knew she had a good heart right from the start. If there were bicycles waiting at a crossing she would always let them go first.

I was undiscovered and alone until one zero temperature night it happened, she said… 'hello'!

It wasn't so long after that I gave her a candy bar and it wasn't so long after than she gave me a cigarette and a free ride home.

I did lie when I told her I was a salesman selling shoes and such – you see I didn't want her knowing that I worked at Duffy's – it was not a club with a good reputation!

I became so struck on Gloria that I couldn't really see the wood for the trees; inasmuch as I hadn't ever envisaged that naturalistically she had a regular life outside that of being a streetcar driver. That being the case you can appreciate how thoroughly pissed off I was on November 26 to come across some newcomer behind the wheel of Gloria's streetcar. It both scared and alerted me to the unpleasant fact that I knew absolutely damn all about her and, that being the case, I had no inkling of her whereabouts. In the worst possible scenario that she didn't return, I hadn't any notion at all of who Gloria was – period. In not so many words, all I knew about Gloria was far from being enough – except I knew what a void was and what was missing in my life and that's about it.

All men have had their lessons to learn in rejection, yet I hadn't even gotten close enough to Gloria to listen or to learn, in spite of that she still was so endowed with pieces of me.

What if she's not here for two or three nights running? My night only began completely with the arrival of Gloria and her streetcar and ended abruptly as I stepped down from it and gazed stony-eyed as its lights faded off into the night.

The following evening I couldn't even hardly remember the words to some of the songs I was singing; it wasn't as though Duffy's robust clientele would have noticed one bit, but I did. Most songs were old classics that I'd covered many times before, however that particular evening my entire focus was elsewhere.

I'll never forget my stint at Duffy's that evening. It just seemed to wear on and on, much too long; I couldn't wait to finish.

The hat check girl had been persistently dropping hints so I promised to take her for a burger when we closed and I was supposed to be doing that very thing. Having said that, I was instead picking up my spondulicks from the head honcho and hurryingly making haste out of the front door before the subdued clapping had done. I felt slightly ratted regarding breaking my date with Mindy (the hat check girl) despite the rumours about her fidelity to her husband, she was really cute.

The House on Dundas and Vine

The city was bitterly cold that night, felt not unlike a Siberian wind or such. I warrant you that a Loblaws top coat (on sale) ain't no barrier to that raw biting and piercing city wind – don't even imagine different!

It wasn't far to the streetcar pick-up point. The sidewalk seemed to be beckoning along now, each and every step nearer and closer to where Gloria would be in just several minutes – or so my addled brain senselessly thought! I felt perked-up and psyched-up to handle all eventualities just as long as those previously mentioned 'eventualities' brought Gloria along soon – yeah, I felt really positive about the outcome.

After a series of short, sharp knocking the constricted concertina door finally opened. You could have struck me dumb as I looked up at the driver on the far side of the bus – it sure wasn't Gloria!

His phizog was the colour of a dirty floor cloth and as he opened his mouth and spoke his chin glistened with gobspit. For a second or two I was ridiculously riveted to that frozen sidewalk – it was as though I had arrived into some twilight zone where everything had lost its sense of propriety.

"Look kid, I've got a bus full of people headed home so are you getting' on or what?" (fact was the streetcar was at its emptiest that time of night).

"I am looking for someone" I eventually uttered.

"Who you looking for then?" he questioned probingly.

"I'm looking for Gloria – she usually drives this bus" I replied.

He looked down on me with a smug smirk. "What the broad with the freckles all over her pan – what do you want with her then?"

"I want to see her" I added.

"Who wants to see her?" he asked, like I was becoming a thorn in his side!

"I do" I answered tactfully.

By now he was beginning to get shitty. "I'm the driver of this streetcar today kid so anyone that you want to see I have to okay it first – do you get it?"

I could feel myself getting hot under the collar, but tried to restrain it. "I don't reckon it's any of your business bub and I think you need a lesson in manners too".

There was a short, sharp knocking sound as the concertina doors struggled to close. That driver was a last word freak for sure as he hollered from his safe warm seat – "Hey, you sing at Duffy's don't you kid? You sure ain't no Sinatra are you?" He laughed and drove off.

It was a sluggishly long trek home that night through the partially melted snow and ice, but nevertheless it hearkened to a discipline my mum had taught me when I was a brat. "*Resourcefulness*, it's all you need Ricky," she would say, "*Resourcefulness.*"

I'd thought about Gloria a lot and oftentimes when I gazed out of my tiny mullion window I'd imagine her walking out across the parklands to the pinewoods beyond. In times of sadness those magical woods could have such a sobering effect on a person's psyche in the way that each majestic pine swept down to meet the frozen fatal lake. Unafraid like a many-fingered switch broom – cold, green, viridian; intense and life-like. Uninterrupted by time, undaunted by snow, ice or wind – unbedazzled by fog and bitter rain. In a landscape of conicalness, from base to crown, not even pretending to be imposing, they just unpretentiously are and will always remain that way.

Here on the far side of time I felt so wounded. For all that I knew Gloria had disappeared forever. Out into the portals of pre-history where it all began. Out where so many ships that passed in the night could flounder, or possibly just across the street, because 'gone' is gone and that's all there was to it!

Of course, I knew that I had become even more of a pathetic mug by bandying words with the new streetcar driver – a silly gamble of sorts; that's all it was.

Philosophically life would move on and by and by things would eventually return to the way they had been before I met her. It seemed to me that what stuck in my craw the most was that I/we didn't even get the look-in to begin to call it 'love'!

I especially wasn't that thrilled about doing my evening session at Duffy's. I knew Mindy quite well and, therefore, I also knew that the second I walked into Duffy's, on seeing me 'still alive' would set things moving fast, inasmuch as an earful of prolonged and loud and louder expletives were going to be heading my way – nobody, but nobody gave Mindy the elbow!

Amid all of that fracas I was also quite likely to get one of the infamous dressing downs by poker-faced Ernestine De Roche who held the title of intermediate kingpin to the whole shady shebang. Ms De Roche insisted that all acts hobnobbed with customers around the bar after they had 'showcased'. It was all just another way of selling more booze before last orders were called.

How could I ever not remember the mucus besmirched features of the streetcar driver? His expression indicated beyond doubt that he wasn't ever going to feel so inclined to let me ride his bus again. Most probably we would exchange third fingers and then I'd be trekking home in the snow once more.

With all of this uncertainty going down you may be wondering why doesn't RD just quit his job at Duffy's as he obviously does not enjoy working there and just maybe another venue would be less disparaging and more appreciative? If the truth be told RD is a prime example of a youngish singer who consistently under estimates himself, and the reason being is not from a musical standpoint as you might have assumed, but tragically permeates from a medical fact.

Question: What can a singer with vocal granuloma do?

Answer: Accept a regular spot at Duffy's and think himself damned lucky!

To be quite candid, Duffy's clique of pie-eyed, juiced-up losers, well they couldn't tell the difference between a singer being artistic or autistic in any event! That ill-mannered streetcar driver didn't realise how accurate his sarcastic Sinatra-esque observation really was – or perhaps he caught my act on a painful day and absolutely did realise I was crappy.

My setback originated years before, inasmuch that I'd never studied formally in the healthy use of my voice and it seemed to me that all of those smoky environments didn't help stop the risk of infection to my throat. However, I still had all of the style and the zip and zing, but my voice per se in the form of a song had long been declining for some time. Most performances had me spraying those evil nodules with lidocaine down inside my throat and sometimes into my nose – trouble being it was only temporarily sustaining at best.

Be that as it may, let us bypass and fast forward all of the barkers of cursed doom and gloom and relate to you what happened later on that evening, as follows:

I am climbing the steps of the last bus home, waiting to have my balls chewed off by the sanctimonious driver at any minute when there, right behind the wheel was Gloria (my Gloria, I hasten to add!). She looked as delicious as buttercream topping and was grinning at me from ear to ear! Demonstratively she sniffed and asked in a particularly childish voice "Did you miss me Ricky?" I felt like responding *"Yes, yes, yes, yes!"* but I heard myself reply "Can I take you for a burger later Gloria?"

Those magical pinewoods may have heard my wishful thinking – I thought they just might – eventually!

3

Gloria's story

Ricky graciously rode my streetcar as if he was a regular downtowner – even assisted some Sisters of Mercy who were struggling with their bags and belongings – just like the Pope incarnate!

After some time I'd finally completed my shift and you could actually see the relief in his eyes to debark that streetcar and walk away from the depot with me. He had gathered up all of the charm he possessed for this occasion and never stopped talking as he escorted me the several blocks to the 'Chicken Roost' – a somewhat dependable den of iniquitous 'pig-outs'!

He was most obviously an established 'regular' to the 'Roost' due to its whereabouts – being next door to Duffy's. Incidentally, the one thing I had learned mighty quickly about Ricky was that he was a lousy liar. It couldn't have occurred to poor Ricky that his tale about him being a shoe salesman was not going to hold water whilst his picture was splashed on the wall outside of Duffy's!

I didn't really care and, in fact, it actually endeared me to him in a maternal type of way, or perhaps it was the fact that Ricky was just too unsophisticatedly honest to be a great story teller. A typical example might be that after he had gone through a great deal of effort to convince and assure me that he, RD was just a regular shoe salesman, he proceeded to remove his shabby top coat to unveil a garish stage suit underneath!

"That's a mighty fine suit for shoe salesmaning" says I, trying to conceal my snarky discourse.

"It's a real gimcrack of a suit isn't it – the only article of any value I possess" says he, with a sniff of snide in his voice.

"I guess I was alluding to the mother-of-pearl buttons festooned to your lapels and shimmying down the sides of your pants" says I, in an animated tone of disbelief.

"It's what the more discerning customers go for" says he, loosening his tie.

"I've never encountered any 'discerning' customers at Duffy's!" says I, smiling smugly from ear to ear.

"So, you sussed me out. You American women are such harridans given half the chance" says he dismissively.

"Not harridans Ricky, we are just a little more on the ball than your European women, not to mention more liberated and vastly more glamorous!" says I staunchly.

Gloria was on a roll now. "If you are looking for somewhat languorous passivity in a woman, go back to Europe Ricky and consider yourself smothered. Lana Turner herself was the power behind the Schwabs drugstore myth – not the producer who supposedly saw her. In Europe the girl would still be sat on the soda fountain stool contemplating her navel!"

"You are vastly different, that part is undoubtedly true and I don't care who wears the pants" says he with all the tenderness he can muster. Ricky was incapable of uttering another single word and Gloria knew it. "The time has come for me to gather up all of my trust and show you, like you have shown me, my only article of any value dear Ricky!"

"Put your coat back on Ricky, goin' to take you to my friend Sammy's garage. It's only about two blocks from Duffy's"

Sammy was still working when Gloria and Ricky arrived at

his garage. Encircled by a multifarious collage of beat-up motor vehicles and wearing the greasiest overalls imaginable!

"Hi Sammy, this is Ricky. He sells shoes and such." Gloria flippantly remarked.

"Yea, I've seen him around" Sammy replied unmoved.

"This used to be my dad's garage Ricky and when he died he left the whole caboodle to Sammy. Sammy had been dad's top mechanic for over thirty years. Dad only asked for one condition, and that was that I could store my legacy in Sammy's garage indefinitely, and here it is!" she added pulling the sackcloth awning off a vehicle in the far corner of the garage.

Gloria looked at me, Sammy looked at me and I looked at the most awesome piece of mean machinery this side of heaven. To wit – a 1941 Buick 8 convertible – all I could add was "hot dog!"

Gloria broke my gawk by adding "It once belonged to Ida Lupino's half-sister who used to be my dad's personal assistant. Sadly, their relationship came to an abrupt end when dad's accountant discovered she had been misappropriating a whole bunch of his greenbacks – she offered the Buick in recompense and dad accepted – good deal huh?"

4

Our story

Mid-week picnics, minding our temper in traffic and listening to the story of one another's life in deadly detail – whatever time it takes, we had that time. Time to be bored, time to be patient and understand, time to watch flowers open all the way – we had all the time we needed.

Just the three of us – Pi, Gloria and Ricky – all on our way to somewhere and all of us speaking at once. Each of us having committed the magnificent error of trusting and caring for the other – separately and altogether. All the while so grateful that we knew how different we were from the standard fare of friends and folks in general – different from what we wondered – yet didn't really care for an answer!

When decidedly Gloria happened to unmothball that fabulous Buick 8, she also decided to give it a name, and that name was 'Passion' because, she says "Passion doesn't need the wind behind it to push it along – passion is a need unto itself – like us, the three of us!"

On this third day of June, riding down the 401 – going where? Going anywhere!

All of us living and breathing the fresh new air of our much-lived in lives and growing stronger and more igneous by the hour.

The House on Dundas and Vine

At that precise moment Mike's 747 was taxiing to the terminal building at Idlewild. We, unknowingly, so unmindful that our nursling of three was about to become four!

5

Mike's story, as told by Ricky

The Tarot is a set of somewhat 'pretentious' cards that nevertheless have an exceptionally long history. There are claims that they derive from the Ancient Egyptians, while others tell of them being European in origin, perhaps around the period of the Crusades.

Pentacles, cups, swords, wands, a Wheel of Fortune, The Hanged Man – Mike knew each one intimately.

Death, The Sun, The Hermit, The Chariot, Strength and World Judgement, The Moon (of course), The High Priestess, The Knight, The Empress, Temperance, The Star, The Tower, The Devil and The Fool! Luther also knows each one intimately.

Mike, or Luther as he prefers to be known, knows the Tarot backwards, and for what it is. He will answer your questions with a sincerity you will swallow hook, line and sinker. The chances are you may find his exhaustive expositions a little bewildering, but that's par for the course – withal you wouldn't expect something so profound to be simple now, would you?

I like to watch Mike shuffling the deck, a procedure quite eye-catching in its own right! Once as he was preparing to lay the cards out, I asked him to give me his thoughts on the intricacies and the subtleties of Tarot readings. Mike stared at me with that impish, cheeky defiant look of his (that would often get him a hiding when we were kids) and replied:

"It's a load of old bollocks Ricky – an out and out load of old bollocks – that's what Tarot readings are!"

Mike's 'performance' and indeed the public's perception of clairvoyance wasn't likely to change in any New York minute – pun intended! From the second his size 12s touched the tarmacked runway at Idlewild his whole demeanour was transmogrified to 'Luther' the mystic(al).

Radio host Bob Grant's lackey Joey had been waiting hours in anticipation of Luther's arrival and now had positioned himself in the Arrival Lounge holding up a hugely becoming placard with 'Luther' emblazoned upon it. Joey reflected on how unnecessary it was, withal Luther had the ability to see him even without the placard – why get in a stew over someone who can communicate with the living and the dead?

Mike smiled at the bullshit of it all. Tomorrow it would be Johnny Carson's Tonight Show and certain as a centipede with all systems working, he would concuss their asinine brain cells – at least that's the way he planned it.

It was a happy day in heaven when I received a phone call from my brother Mike saying that he was back in N.Y. and had agreed to sit for an interview with Radio host Bob Grant. We agreed to meet up the day after – for my kid brother Mike I could get ready on real short notice.

He answered the door to his brownstone apartment on 68th Street looking nothing like Luther, but a lot like my dear ill-groomed brother. He held me tight in a big bear hug and then began to show me around his four-room apartment. Small kitchen with a few worn and mucky appliances, a bedroom dominated by an unmade bed, a bathroom whose toilet was constantly running and a living room that was furnished like a set for a way-off Peter Cushing movie. All around the living room were dog-eared paperbacks and coffee-stained hardbacks from Crowley to Thomas Harris to William Shatner no less!

Between the apartment and a few restaurants we talked a lot, often into the early hours of the morning. He'd often lie on the couch and occasionally jump up and go into the kitchen to light us a couple of Camel blues from the stove.

One night as we were retiring to bed I smelled something burning which was kind of disconcerting living on the eighth floor. We ran into the kitchen to see a tea towel and part of the kitchen worktop in flames. Mike just calmly picked up the kettle and doused the fire out as if such occurrences happened all the time!

I had of course contacted Gloria and Pi regarding the arrival of Mike and met them at Penn Station a couple of days later. They were really excited at the prospect of finally meeting our Mike – they had heard so many stories about his misadventures. Mike had arranged to get us all front seats to see him on the Johnny Carson Tonight Show. Johnny's other guest was Shirley MacLaine who was playing the part of a hooker in a movie called Irma la Douce.

Dear Mike, my kid brother, he was one of a kind. Splendidly spruced up and sprawled out on Johnny Carson's chesterfield with a quite flirtatious Ms MacLaine next to him. With his beautiful long blonde hair and expressive necklaces, rings and bracelets that rattled when he moved, he really looked like he owned the show – and in a supercilious way, he did!

He had come an awful long way since telling sloshed women their fortunes in crummy Bournemouth discotheques and locating dead spouses for folks in retirement homes … *viva la difference*, my Mike!

Years later I remember Gloria saying to me "I cannot remember what life was like the day before Mike came." That sentiment spelt it out for me too!

We all didn't feel particularly crowded in Mike's apartment, although there was a more than average surge for the bathroom in the early a.m. However, after all of the jovialities that N.Y. had to offer, we were pleased to be heading back to Dundas and Vine again – with a persuadable Mike in tow!

6

Free rein

There is not one single day or time of day in my thus far life that I'd want to change or alter. In the six months that I've been living here with my Gloria, my Pi and my Mike here on the mountain at The House on Dundas and Vine. I suspect that being here I don't as yet realise the true significance of where I am and what has taken place. I cannot even speculate on the enormity of what we have all established together, except to say that being here together is the nourishment that we all desperately needed for all of us had agreed that too many endless winters alone was not good for the soul.

It's kind of nice too to know, and not to be afraid to speak of, love by its first name and to live love by its last – viz not to be afraid of what's upcoming and not to be afraid of what's gone before. Even the darkness at the top of the stairs and the apprehension of what might lay in wait around the corner seemed to be more optimistic, more friendly and indeed more valuable. The old notion of knowing exactly where life was going didn't seem important any longer. Maybe in some respect you may argue that life should have some sort of game plan and should, therefore have some sort of rough idea of where it's going – relax, game plans seldom work out in any event – do they?

Here at The House on Dundas and Vine all that we wanted from one another was our names, not our reputations. It's a silly fact, and even as I sing our praises, I realise that when you reach a certain age it's difficult to keep all of your skeletons in the cupboard. It's as though those boned up combatants of yesteryear demand to be awakened. Remember, it's so easy to end a new beginning with your misplaced values and so keep those cupboards locked. Conscience is a fool's domain at best!

The way I figure it is that if Canada was tipped upside down all of southern Ontario would land up in Hudson Bay, but what would it achieve? Stay shtum regarding the past, there is nothing compatible about it. At The House on Dundas and Vine you don't need to air old values. Here it's enough after a while to say goodbye to them for good.

7

Hootenanny v Rock n Roll!

We had so many hootenannies at The House on Dundas and Vine and yet I still remember with ease every single one. Cider, cigars and breadsticks always spring to mind. Neckties and petticoats with red, red roses in our buttonholes seem like only moments ago.

Pi would strum hard and fast upon an old Goya steel-string she'd picked up at a Lower East pawn shop forming the basic G, C and D chords she'd learned from Mike.

Gloria had a sweet clear voice, even higher than Joan Baez's soaring soprano.

Mike had fallen in love with an ancient 3-string double bass that used to belong to Gloria's father. Me – I did an awful lot of clapping and kept the glasses topped up!

When I first arrived in Canada I used to frequent the Half Note Club in Toronto. Sitting at the bar on a balmy evening with a G&T and a meatball sandwich was about as close to paradise as I had ever gotten – until now. The House on Dundas and Vine taught me a lot differently!

It was still quite early in the a.m. and yet we were very much up and about. Indeed, Gloria had percolated another pot of Chase and Sanborn and was bringing us sweet rolls and an enormous slice of the cake that she had baked the day before.

Whenever our Mike was home for a long weekend there had to be 'cake', you could guarantee it.

It was the third day of the Cuba crisis and the standoff continued. Pi was convinced that the world was about to destroy itself. Her fears had been growing when on October 15 a U.S. spy plane had discovered missiles in Cuba. To date there was a military blockade of the island in place. "Sure to be challenged soon!" she said cynically. It took Mike to snap her out of her melancholy by enquiring whether she would prefer to go to a James Brown or Sam Cooke concert the next time he returned to N.Y.? Pi was beaming big time, but replied that she would prefer to go to "one of them gospel shindigs where all the black Sheilas are swaying from side-to-side hollering 'save me sweet Jesus'."

Pi nearly fell off the kitchen chair she was sitting on with hysterical laughter when right out of the blue Mike began to demonstrate his unique version of the 'twist' and yelling "save me sweet Jesus" at the same time!

Pi had peculiar tastes. Perhaps they stemmed from her Australian roots? One thing was for sure, she was drawn compatibly to Mike. They really were both on the same wavelength. Mike had always been a ground breaker when it came to discovering further rainbows when the near ones faltered or faded. "I am kind of outgrowing rock n roll per se" he untruthfully asserted. He then looked around at all of us and scoffed "do you know, I am the only one who wears a regular suit and is under thirty years of age at N.Y. clubs. The new set that are making the scene are all much older folk dressed in tuxedos and tit protruding dresses!"

All of that to one side, Mike's 'piece de resistance' to Pi didn't really take too much thought. "Your choice Pi – Bobby Darin at the Copacabana or Ricky Dale at Duffy's Tavern? A difficult decision I know, but it's up to you" he said with a big smirk aimed toward me!

For all of the diplomatic brinkmanship and threats of but-ton-pushing that were played out in late 1962, the Cuban Missile Crisis often returns to me with such a feeling of fondness and affection, particularly when I hear the coffee start to perk and the smell of sweet rolls and cake permeates and overindulges my senses – a personal perspective of course!

8

"Free at last"

August 28, 1963 was quite an eventful day that we'll likely never know again.

Brother Mike and me headed out to Washington D.C. in the wee small hours to join the other 250,000 souls gathered at the Lincoln Memorial. Whilst we strained like hell to hear Martin Luther King, Jr. sing out his dream of freedom and equality, I wouldn't swap that day for all the silver in Sacramento. In some long-forgotten time, some July or August, even then we'll talk about the times gone by today.

Mike decided we'd stay in his apartment for a few days in order to get our emotional stamina back, but right now in the steamy Washington heat all I could think about was an ice- cold coke and a shower.

Just on the far side of 68th Street we were really beginning to shrivel up when out of the blue we found ourselves surrounded by a group of wrathful black youths who were in no mood for brotherhood!

"You's know who dat is, don't you guys?" declared the Brob-dingnagian fella to his half-cocked rooters.

"Yea, yea of course I remember now, you dat English wizard dude on Carson's Show the other night." This was the runt of the pack speaking. I liked him, he didn't seem like too much trouble.

"Nice of you to drop by" says Mike with his eyes on each one in turn. I too was beginning to soak up the body language and wondered whether this may be a fight or flight situation.

Mike had kept his distance from the pack, but at the same time he began nudging a little closer to the big fella – he was the one that Mike was eyeing. I began to be really concerned now, not necessarily for our well-being, but for the well-being of the kids. Mike had made a defence video in the U.K. several years ago. It was called 'Self Defence That Works'. It was based upon skills he had learned whilst living in Okinawa. The video had been almost immediately banned due to the use of the words 'self defence'. The skills contained in the video were skills on how to debilitate or, worse still, eliminate a 'would be' attacker – for good!

"I saw you pull needles out your mouth" said this funny looking little guy with a wonky eye.

"I remember dat you said you had sex wid a gorilla too" – they had all joined in the conversation now.

Mike all of a sudden stepped in fast and close to the big guy and in a flash pulled a flapping pigeon from out of the guy's half-zipped baseball jacket – just like that!!

It was as though he had pole-axed them all. Buggered and be-witched they applauded and then as quickly as they had arrived, they had gone – in a kind of whirlwind of awe and amazement and, perhaps, fear!

"If you can't beat 'em, join 'em" Mike looked at me and smiled like a cheeky insolent kid. I knew what he meant, he had an intuitive way of staying on the right side of language and the black side of magic!

"It's all about displacement" Mike said kind of insidiously and then suddenly his alter ego seemed to take over as I'd seen often happen before.

"It's kind of ironic after listening to Dr King today that you can just take a person's unacceptable violent urge and channel it accordingly without them ever knowing. For example Ricky, I only know enough about myself as yet to know that I don't know enough. Nor can I say what's missing in me – voids are voids and only seen completely for what they are after we've had victories over them. Dr King is an optimist in any event as he believes that man has the capacity to do right as well as wrong and that ultimately our path is upwards, not downward."

"A bit like kick the dog instead of the boss and you may be looked upon more favourably" says I.

"In a way" says Mike "an often-used displacement remedy is punching your pillow, since by venting your anger that way you are less likely to hit anybody else."

"Mike, I think you've been out to lunch with the fairies again, but so what!" says I. "Just tell me one thing, where did you get that pigeon from and how did it come to be under that guy's coat?"

Meanwhile, back at The House on Dundas and Vine:-

Pi was thrilled to have received a letter confirming she had been awarded an International Student Scholarship to join the fall program at McMaster University in Hamilton. Gloria was going through all the technicalities of driving the new electric trolley buses – dear old streetcars were being pensioned off at last!

9

Rocker panels?

Gloria was a fruitcake when it came to watching soap operas on the tv. Her favorite by far was 'The Patty Duke Show'. The two main characters in the show were identical cousins, both of course played by Patty. Special effects being relatively primitive in those days, meant that each time the zany, all-American, forever 'in a fix' but good-hearted Patty faced the camera to talk to her prim Scottish cousin Cathy, someone had to stand with her back to the camera and pretend to be Cathy and when it was Cathy's turn to show face, someone had to play Patty!

It wasn't often that Gloria and me shared the same day off work. Be that as it may, we were both not due into work until evening time. As soon as the credits came up on the Patty Duke Show we were both heading out to Loblaws at Stoney Creek to choose our winter coats together.

Backing the 1941 Buick 8 convertible into a Loblaw's parking space, designed for lesser vehicles, was difficult and by and by a loud metallic clunk was heard! Within seconds a furious Italian woman, who was pure unadulterated hayseed, appeared. Gloria got out of the car noting that the damage I had done to the other car was slight.

"You and your Buick" the woman yelled at me "someone's going to pay for this!"

By now a crowd of curious onlookers had gathered as the woman threw her arms about and jabbered away incoherently in her own language.

"Look lady!" Gloria said meaningfully, and took a small decorative sheet of paper from her bag and signed it. "Take this across to Sammy's Repair Shop on Dufferin Street and he'll fix your car up and bill me."

The crowd dispersed and the enraged woman got back into her car without batting an eyelid and skedaddled in a hurry.

"You know who that was don't you Ricky?" Gloria said smiling rather smugly. "Her name is Francesca Controni – grande dame to Guiseppe (Pep) Controni et al. She owns the Pines Restaurant in Stoney Creek. We should go there one evening. You'd like it."

"Here's the thing Ricky – if you are going to play 'dodgems' then Francesca Controni's black Cadillac is the perfect choice."

I was slightly puzzled and allowed Gloria to continue.

"I knew that the chances were zero of her getting the bump fixed – not with about fifty kilos of refined white stuff stowed away in the rocker panels. Did you see how low to the road that car was? Ask yourself Ricky, would you like to leave your car overnight in Sammy's Repair Shop?"

I smiled knowingly, but wasn't certain that what Gloria had told me was a source of comfort or not – perhaps of sorts it was!

IO

"Every new beginning comes from some other beginning's end"

When I subconsciously eyeball Gloria as she walks across the room, or when we're alone and I gaze intently into her burnt sienna eyes, it's as though the whole shebang of cloud cuckoo land daydreams I've ever had or ever read about Canada are suddenly in tune. Just her impressive presence epitomises that she is the prerequisite that I needed to becoming a Canadian proper.

Seems like long ago now, but during the fall of '58 I had unequivocally set my sights on relocating to southern Ontario. A couple of years before my dad had died in a mining tragedy just outside the town of Sault Ste Marie. Mom, my younger brother Mike and me had been putting money to one side so that after a bit we could all afford to visit dad's grave and the location where he died. Mom passed away – it was as though she had given up the ghost – her heart just gave up too.

Mike and me chose not to attend mom's funeral, not because of irreverence. I guess it was our refusal to accept being knocked back again.

Mike uppercut his teacher and totally unconcerned he walked out of school. I packed our suitcases and within 24 hours we were bound for Montreal on the maiden voyage of RMS Franconia. Mom and Canada were deep-rooted in our psyche. This is what she would have wished for us.

Montreal was such a haven of activity and, as youthful adolescents, we very quickly fell hopelessly in love with the whole great ambiance of the city.

We found an apartment on Clark Street, just off the main drag with a front and back balcony view of the streets. The rent was outrageously cheaper than the U.K. and it wasn't long before we'd both found reasonably paid jobs earning considerably more than kids of our age would have earned in those dismal decades back in the U.K.

Mike and I were both very resourceful kids. We exaggerated our ages and experience and, together with some 'round the clock' footslogging, the streets of Montreal took us in.

There seemed to be an abundance of single women in 1960s Montreal and I surely knew that it wouldn't be long before my brother Mike became acquainted. He met his 'Mrs Robinson' at the Quebec Winter Carnival – which basically is a party in the snow – as if summer didn't exist! She was vacationing at Jean Chretien's home, who had just been elected to Parliament, and so was away for several days. Apparently, she plied Mike with an abundance of caribou cocktails (red wine + whiskey + a dash of maple syrup!) and he replied quite enthusiastically!

As a kid Mike was torn between being Jim Stark (Rebel Without a Cause) and Aleister Crowley. With regard to Crowley, Mike had read a whole shelf of stuff about him and all of that jiggery pokery and, as Mike grew older, he began to put it to some good use. It's where his spiritual vocationing suddenly came into its own!

When Mike was a little kid he was frequently getting up to mischief and mom often had to whack him. She had this wooden pole that she used for poking down the washing in the boiler and on one of Mike's badly behaved occasions she broke it on him. You have to remember that dad was away in the Sault and

Mike's so-called 'mischief' was not just impish behaviour. On one occasion he set the woods on fire and on another he dug a hole in the lounge floor looking for treasure! Mom would shout and call him 'a fiend from hell' and Mike never disappointed her label.

In any event Mike's 'Mrs Robinson' was not averse to some ill-disposed satanic 'magick' (as Crowley spelled it). The more ceremonial the better! As far as Mike was concerned every cultist needed a hobby and his was insanely wealthy women. By such time that he had exponentially reawakened her spiritual self, interpreting the Tarot to her was just a purgatorial aftershock and a precursor to do it all again!

Mike had a cherubic smirk on his face when he proudly told me that she unquestionably accepted he was 'the devil incarnate'; we both of us agreed that it had a somewhat nice commercial sound and was definitely an improvement on merely being 'a fiend from hell'.

It seemed likely that 'Mrs Robinson's' subsequent yatter amongst the well-heeled loons of Montreal society could have been a huge factor in putting Mike on the 'most wanted to meet' map – the rest they say is pure history.

Dear Mike. He's come the distance since setting the woods on fire and it's mostly due to his brass-necked charm which will always outshine conventional better judgement ... that, and the fact that his mojo never stopped working!

As for Ricky Dale! I was nearly always just a few steps short of some stage door, but there were always those cheapskates who wanted to hire a reliable 'middle of the road' entertainer for peanuts! After a few weeks of merciless auditioning and put-downs, I finally wound up singing full-time in the chic cocktail lounge of D'Agostino's former establishment in the fashionable downtown district of the city.

I felt an air of quality working here. Very few people could gainsay that Ricky Dale didn't possess a certain wholesome forte, and if the tone-deaf were to indolently interrupt the continuity of my performances they were instantaneously put out in the street by two tuxedo giants!

However, my most advantageous stroke of luck was that the proprietress, who turned out to be Rocco Zito's mom, found me 'endearing'. The fact that I'd grasped a handful of the Sicilian[1] lingo really was very beneficial. I knew better than to mention that *Ndrangheta* was also a word that I understood extremely well too!

It seemed to me that genuine singing talent wasn't always the best way in which an artist could fulfil the equation – just knowing when to keep your mouth shut as well was by far the most advantageous!

Mike was so exhilarated after being offered a character role in the children's television romp 'The Randy Dandy Show'. It was our assumption that he would naturally take on the specific role of Captain Randy Dandy, but it soon became apparent that Mike's discernible role was that of the Captain's team mate, Silly Willy Clown.

There was no avoiding the actuality that Captain Randy was required to speak fluent French, whereas Silly Willy merely said things like 'whoosh', 'whoopee' and habitually tumbled around and got knocked to the ground and got squirmed upon by two impish make-believe eels called Ethel and Egburt! It was all too much of a kick back for poor Mike. The reality was that he was also getting pissed off with shagging his lady friend to order!

Unlike me, Mike was never a freak of musicals. He did however go ape over 'West Side Story'. He knew all the dialogue and songs off by heart. When Mike began dating he'd often falsify

---

1 During his early childhood Ricky spent time in Calabria whilst his father was undertaking essential engineering work near Mt Etna

his name. His phoney most liked were Riff (of course), A-Rab and Tiger. From time to time he'd expect his then girl friends to also take on a West Side moniker such as Velma, Clarice or Francisca. I guess that's the reason why after cracking all his nuts in Montreal, the Big Apple beckoned and endorsed all of Mike's imaginings head-on.

There's something due
any day;
I will know
right away;
Soon as it shows
I got a feeling there's a miracle due
gonna come true
Bright as a rose…

Mike and I – we were such cockleburrs in those wilful heydays of our youth. It surely was a miracle that some Italianate person didn't stop our farting in church once and for all. I look back in abject amazement at those dazzling days when oftentimes our day-to-day involvements weren't made up of just dodging pigeons in the square. That would have been too simple for us!

We were the first-hand visionaries to what we saw as the rapidly mushrooming beginning of what became known as 'the Palermo Spring' (a tense calm where Cosa Nostra killers were under orders to lie low). A Spring that no one else saw coming, no one noticed when it did come and no one could possibly say when it would end! When things like that happen behind the scenes it becomes difficult to close a blind eye and better by far to just move off in a different direction entirely before 'your' plug is pulled!

The House on Dundas and Vine

"Morning gentlemen! Nice day for a murder!"

James Cagney – Angels With Dirty Faces

II

Aunt Laura

I had a somewhat formal invitation to lunch today. I say formal because it was characterized by a visit from two herculean, unsmiling henchmen with shoulders not dissimilar to Robert Mitchum. By all accounts Mrs Zito Snr had requested my company pronto! She lived alone in an elegant townhouse on the fringe of Rue Jean-Talon.

As I pulled up cautiously outside I was greeted by a husky blonde lady in gardening gloves who was pruning a small bush. "Naw, you couldn't be Ricky Dale – you are too young! You can call me Aunt Laura – go on in. You are expected!"

I spent a marvellous afternoon with Aunt Laura and Mrs Zito Snr, who liked me to refer to her as 'mom'. She had carefully organised a whole bundle of old photographs of the family and Aunt Laura translated Mom Zito's spoken account of each one.

The gist of my invite suddenly began to become apparent when Mom Zito let it be known (by way of Aunt Laura) that she didn't care to live in Montreal full stop! She said it had become an unacceptable way of living for her for some time and she had a longing to return to Hamilton. She said that Hamilton was where she was raised after her folks had landed here from Calabria. I started to become concerned when she quite bro-

ken-heartedly related that Montrealers had been 'molesting her'!
Aunt Laura briskly came to the rescue of Mom Zito's broken
English and explained to me that what she intended to express
was the locals couldn't get their tongue around the name 'Zito'
and pronounced it as 'Zither'. They had not been, as Mom had
so worryingly put it, 'molesting' her. Regrettably Rocco hadn't
listened to Aunt Laura's accurate translation and had cracked
a few heads unnecessarily just the same! However, the general
purpose of my invitation to their home was that Mom Zito
wanted to bring me along to their new home, which by all accounts was on the fringes of Hamilton and called Stoney Creek.
I was eager and really quite chuffed – by all accounts the Zito
family owned and ran an abundance of impressively smart and
fashionable establishments both in Hamilton and Toronto. Yes,
you could say that I was 'cock a hoop' with the proposition!

Looking back on that phase of Mike's and my lives here in
North America I cannot remember even one single day that
we'd want to have altered. Possibly there were some days along
the way that we could have missed, but I suspect that we could
not have arrived where we are today in any different way. The
misgivings that I have are that being here in this extemporized
so-called nirvana, neither Mike nor me knew exactly where we
were yet.

From time to time I heard bad things about my newsworthy
closeness with the Zito family. They are oftentimes referred to
as being a 'Mafia' family. It seemed to me that 'Mafia' had become almost a cliché, an umbrella label for a long lot of words
like pizza, spaghetti, opera and a whole world panoply of gangs
and criminals far, far beyond Sicily. I saw it as merely an Italian
language given to many other languages across the world. Especially in the United States where the 'Mafia' in the strict sense of
the word were purported to be based.

Moulded fame. Modulated wealth and muddled identity – it's true that there was an element of uncertainty regarding some of the clandestine, so-called 'activities' of my new friends. I believe that it is cinematic stylized nonsense that helped to create attention to those 'activities' that were often time quite honourable and virtuous and speaking ill of them does us no credit at all.

My affable new friends were an association of folk who collectively are referred to as 'Ndrangheta'. They originated from Calabria in the Italian 'toe' and are in fact a much older association than said 'Mafia'. The quasi-simplistic notion that 'Ndrangheta' kill people and get away with it because, by definition, they are Sicilian is as unrealistic as saying Al Pacino must be Mafioso because he played Michael Corleone – although perhaps it's not such an anomaly after all … you choose!

12

Mike's confession

*A fellow will remember a lot of things you wouldn't think
he'd remember. Years ago I was crossing over to Jersey on the
ferry and as we pulled out there was another ferry pulling in
and on it there was a girl waiting to get off. A white dress
she had on, she was carrying a white parasol. I only saw her
for one second. She didn't see me at all, but I'll bet a month
hasn't gone by since that I haven't thought of that girl*

Citizen Kane (the movie)

Everyone else had sensibly gone to bed and there was just Mike
and me sat by the hearth enjoying the remains of the log fire
and chugalugging the remains of black cherry bourbon. It's odd
how drowsiness, infused with the right quantity of alcohol, can
often bring out the best in a person.

Mike looked across at me. I could detect there was a soberly
sincere look upon his face.

"Have you ever been in love Ricky? Yea you have! There was
that Dutch tulip girl wasn't there? Well, I am in love too!"

I looked at Mike suspiciously, not really convinced that this
wasn't going to turn out as some kind of joke. "Since when
Mike?"

Mike looked back at me plainly miffed.

"Since you first invited me to this so-called 'House on Dundas and Vine'… I feel restless, dizzy and I can't sleep at night."

Trying not to be too flippant I replied "Dear ol' Mike – it sounds like indigestion to me!"

Mike just stared expressionlessly into the dying embers of the fire. It was almost as though he had become embarrassed by disclosing stuff to me and replied like there was a thorn in his side. "Love don't make things nice Ricky. It ruins everything! It makes things a mess and it breaks hearts. People think love is perfection. It isn't! Only snowflakes and stars are perfection; love is bullshit."

I put my arm around my little brother's massive shoulders and mumbled "Hell Mike, you really are in love aren't you – you wanna tell me who?"

13

And so on, and so forth . . .

Pi has been elected senior member of the Student Faculty
Council and apparently narrates non-stop love poetry as she
goes about her domestic duties

— Christina Rossetti, 'A Birthday' and others!

Gloria says she thinks the new electric buses are an abomination, however, that isn't to admit that she doesn't get a buzz out of driving them.

Mike has his own mid-morning slot on New York's Channel 7, tutoring folks on sexual deviancy and such. He visits us every weekend and parks his 125mph Vincent Black Shadow out front so's the neighbours can admire! A piece of art to be revered indeed!!

Ricky is still painstakingly serenading downtown drunks at Duffy's and has taken to ice sculpting a figurine on a piece of frozen ground next to the house.

And what of The House on Dundas and Vine? It's prepossessing, it's where we all assemble. The hill above it is either summer green or spotless white – the sky a constant foggy blue from the smoggy, smooth atmosphere of the city below. The House on Dundas and Vine is needy of us and we of it. However, not at all does it change, only we have that abject ability!

She brought me marmalade and toast for my breakfast and I was all at once aware that her footsteps across the kitchen floor had become sacramental.

14

Part one : Cuddly winter nights

It was by far the bestest summer I had ever had. We'd all go to the lake in the '41 Buick – roof back 'n Chuck Berry – 'You Never Can Tell'. We all swam a lot and I even grew slightly tanned. All of us had really grown that summer of '64, Mike, Gloria, me and Pi too!

It was now early October and the Indian summer we were experiencing was showing signs of coming to an end. The sky was becoming crabby, the maples, oaks and ashes had turned dark red, brown and yellow and overall the whole countryside was so hurtfully beautiful to the eye. The bunch of conifers up on the hill overseeing The House on Dundas and Vine seemed to stand over us like a bunch of disapproving mannequins looking out on the street; that somewhat formidable evergreen was in a class of its own! Most of the secondary roads and sidewalks in and around our House on Dundas and Vine were absolutely carpeted with fallen leaves. Pi remarked that they made a lovely gay crackling sound as you hoofed your way through them "like walking through oodles of cornflakes" she said – and she was right!

It was around 10pm and Gloria and I were doing our bedtime ablutions. I, in fact, had already taken root! In a few minutes Gloria appeared at the bedroom door in her bathrobe carrying her streetcar matching apparel over her arm.

"I need to iron this before I come to bed Ricky – it wasn't dry enough this morning."

"That's OK" I replied "my time is yours me darling."

Gloria walked over to the socket by the window and plugged in the iron. "Look!" she cried excitedly "it's snowing hard!"

I immediately jumped out of bed and went over to see for myself. "Whadda ya know!" I said.

She turned with a big smile toward me "First snow this year!"

"Yeah" I said, putting my arms around her and kissing the nape of her neck "First this year!"

In a moment her gentle arms were around me too, then unexpectedly she dropped them. "The iron must be hot by now" she said.

"So indeed am I Gloria" I replied "like a lovelorn calf." She sniggered and tested the iron on a handkerchief. "Not warm enough Ricky" she responded. "Says who?" I demanded, purposely misunderstanding her impliance and then sorrowfully adding "I'm boiling over!"

"It's not about you Ricky Dale, it's about the iron." She saw the silly smile on my face, switched the iron off and walked beguilingly toward me like the heavenly angel in human form that she was.

I'd seldom been kissed back with such veracity and acute urgency and couldn't make sense of how we had managed to shift from 'ironing' to my Gloria's honeyed tongue language. That nice looking bathrobe lay somewhat cruelly crumpled on the carpet. I cannot recollect us removing it, only that it had been hiding her naked body and the guarded arcane parts that longed to be rediscovered and caressed.

Her body;
Extemporized
Eroticized
She eyes me;
Wonderingly
Wishfully
I gaze back;
Recklessly
Two mindedly
Poised she hazards;
Certainty
Unquestionably
We touch;
Unthinkingly
Magically
Desire strikes;
Blindingly
Impatiently...

...tangled in passion, pulsing together, touched by a breath, kissed by a whisper, waiting for the imminent shudder, enveloped in the uncontrollable aftershock...
...drained and fulfilled in the meantime – of an instant!

15

Part two : Transcendental

We both lay there for a few moments gazing at the cracked ceiling and reflecting upon how profound sticky speechlessness truly is. Tiny chinks of light were just about beginning to break through the winter drapes and fleck the room like a kaleidoscopic of happenstance to our love-in a twinkling before. Gloria had often speculated on whether or not we had known one another in a previous life. I have to admit that since knowing Gloria I am often of the same mind. In this universe of uncertainty and ambiguity, who's to say how many lifetimes we'd lived previously. Just the off guarded fact that Gloria and I were able to connect in this lifetime is in itself proof enough for me.

In spite of us being rather overcome from the night before, it was Gloria who spoke the first sentence of the day. "Be damned Ricky Dale, my poor legs are so weak this morning from being wrapped around you all night!" She nevertheless managed to totter down the mezzanine to the kitchen and make us some steamy coffee! It had become something of a tradition of late. Coffee and the mandatory 'Lucky Strike' – LSMFT[2] you know!

Back between the sheets, Gloria moseyed up and put her head on my arm. I liked it when she did that!

---

2 Lucky Strike means fine tobacco

"Ricky… do you agree that the old hackneyed expression 'make love' is perhaps a trifle demeaning and outdated?" She looked up from her comfy position with a 'come up with an answer Ricky' expression.

"Yea, I suppose it is" I replied. "What are your thoughts on it sweetheart?" (my 'stop gap' reply!)

She went quiet for a moment or two and then replied "To me Ricky the phrase 'make love' clearly gives the impression that something is being manufactured or perhaps assembled – I think it's a horrible phrase. It takes away all of the 'demonstrative' emotion and leaves a beautiful happening completely flavourless."

I nodded in agreement, but felt that there was a tailpiece to Gloria's observation that was in need of adding – "Perhaps a whole new more precise and elegant language is required" I said optimistically "Rather than 'making love' perhaps we should rename it 'sharing love'!"

Gloria had a genuine partiality for my ad-libbed 'rename'. She wrote it in her daybook straightaway – said the 'rename' was transcendentally quite poetic and I agreed.

We were wide awake now and it was me who raised the revealing question of our Mike being in love and with whom and Gloria was all ears!

She chuckled out loud at first until I straight-faced assured her "It's bona fide Gloria, proper love. I swear I've never ever seen Mike quite so obsessed before."

Gloria held my face between the palms of her hands and stared cautiously and surreptitiously into my eyes. "Do you know the meaning of unrequited love Ricky?" she asked.

I dearly adored my Gloria whenever she was in this kind of reactive mood and returned her question by saying "Sure I do – it means a love that isn't returned."

"Perhaps more Ricky, perhaps more" and with that she took my hand and placed it upon her breast. "Does it feel good Ricky – it feels good to me."

I was at a loss for words – it seemed to me that this was one of those occasions when I should just shut-up and listen!

Gloria continued with her assessment.

"Of course it feels good Ricky, if it didn't then our love would be kind of unrequited, but what if we both wanted to touch, but couldn't because nothing can be returned if the other person doesn't know?"

I looked at her and smiled. "Can I place my other hand on your other breast, or should I ask your permission first sweetheart?"

She looked back at me and smiled too. "You are getting the idea Ricky. With unrequited love no progression can be permitted without explicit spoken consent."

Now Gloria and I were really in tune. "Ricky dear, it only becomes unrequited because it is not openly reciprocated or returned in kind – in other words you are not sure whether they love you back."

Just to let Gloria know 'I got it' I began to finish off the plot thus. "If each beloved is unaware of the other's deep and strong romantic affection it must be really horrible for them. Loving someone who does not, indeed cannot, return those feelings."

Gloria added in agreement "It must be really horrible. Pi has been singing this poem around our house for the past month Ricky –

"My heart is like a singing bird
Whose nest is in a water'd shoot;
My heart is like an apple-tree
Whose boughs are bent with thickset fruit;

My heart is like a rainbow shell
That paddles in a halcyon sea;
My heart is gladder than all these
Because my love is come to me."

Ricky: Christina Rossetti??
Gloria: Yea, I think so!"

The next morning when Mike came downstairs for breakfast he was bewildered to find that Gloria and I were nowhere to be seen. It was particularly unusual to find the kitchen and eating area deserted because it had become our tradition of late that at 9am prompt every Saturday Gloria and I would be rustling up a whole mess of delicious mouth-watering breakfast victuals.

It was due to the fact that every rushed weekday we all had our scripted schedules which dictated to us to 'get a move on'.

Saturday and Sunday mornings were our collaborative 'pig-out' gatherings. We became good for nothing slobs who couldn't recapitulate about calories until Monday morning and it gave us all an extra gusto and enthusiasm to get out of bed as well!

Chewing over what might have happened to us, Mike walked sleuthingly out onto the back porch. He could hear the tiny clicks from last night's snow as the aspiring morning sun began diminishing its frostiness. He listened curiously and faintly, very faintly he could detect the echo of someone practising the chromatic scales on the piano in the summer house.

"Must be Pi" he cogitated and very carefully negotiated his way across the icy compound to the warmth of the small building.

Twas Pi! "Where are Gloria and Ricky for goodness sake? Mike I'm worried, where are they?"

Mike looked at her sat on the piano stool. She was so faultless, so trusting. "I've been behaving in a contemptible and

cheap way Pi and it seems to me that the cat's out of the bag –
Gloria and Ricky have twigged me – they've gone out because
they don't want to see my face again. It's a fitting time for me to
return to N.Y. Pi" he added.

Pi's face was pallid with fear and quiet tears fell unabated
upon the dormant keyboard and then, as if in all out defying,
she snapped "I am coming with you Mike. You are not as young
as you used to be, but it doesn't matter. I love you!" Her voice
was choked in ardent passion when she adamantly added "I lost
my dad, so help me God I am not losing you Michael!"

When an ancient 1941 Buick 8 convertible with gold leaf
signage cued on its tail reading 'Passion' passes by, folks tended
to stop in the street and take notice. When the same pulls into
the driveway of The House on Dundas and Vine, notwithstand-
ing that it's early morning and the whole world is frozen – the
neighbors tended to schozz somewhat!

Pi stood up with a start. "They're back!" she exclaimed, grab-
bing her coat and handbag from a chair. "What are we going to
do Mike, what are we going to do?"

Mike just stood and stared out of the window, stupidly –
with no plan. Just for that moment in time he felt unable to
speak or move. A feeling of total unreality, until his love for Pi
kicked in and embroiled him and sent him topsy-turvy. "We're
going to get married Pi, that's what we are goin' to do" and
then it was almost like he was talking to himself as he chunt-
ered "don't imagine Gloria and Ricky will be any too pleased
and cannot say that I blame them, but I am never going to
walk away from you my Pi – that's just the incredible way this
cookie crumbles!"

It was Gloria who first confronted Mike. "We know all about
you two" she said with a precautionary smile.

Mike bowed his head sheepishly and muttered "How'd you
find out?" His voice was kind of rough and shaky.

"Oh we figured it out Mike – took us a while though."

Gloria's admiration for Mike had always been one hundred per cent genuine in every aspect and now she bathed in it, let it swirl over her. In the catch of the moment she uncloaked that long-drawn admiration with her eyes, voice and thoughts and let him have it all, right between the eyes. Completely and almost methodically their head-to-head became a recondite heart-to-heart and I shared every wonderful syllable she spoke.

"We love you and our Pi so dearly Mike. So much so that your lives have become more central and valuable to us than our own. Ricky will tell you how instantly our hearts flutter in anxiety and dread on each and every occasion you and Pi take the Vincent for a twirl. It's ridiculously like death is on every road and in every other vehicle. Dear Mike, did you and Pi honestly imagine that Ricky and I would be disapproving of your love for each other. Ricky told me about when you and he were kids, your mother would often blackmail the pair of you into eating your meat-filled dinners. Mike, this isn't an 'are you or aren't you' situation where a kiss is often followed by a curse – double entendres are not our way Mike, or indeed yours!"

I'd wanted to add something to what Gloria had said, but on quick reflection I decided she had covered it all. Well, we all got involved with a considerable amount of over emotional hugs and a few too many tears, which I guess was par for the course. It wasn't until Pi piped in with "You still haven't told us where you both disappear too!" That's when the second piece of unintentional unravelling began in earnest. At this juncture it became my prerogative to be shedding some light.

"Several days ago I received a telephone call from Aunt Laura – you may recall, she was Mrs Zito's unofficial translator. Apparently, Mrs Zito Sr took her dogs walking in Gage Park meticulously between 9-10am every Saturday morning. She was always accompanied by Aunt Laura and one of Rocco's henchmen."

"By all accounts Mrs Zito Sr had requested that Gloria and I met her by the war memorial at precisely 9.30am on November 10. I didn't realise until that telephone call that, apart from mine and Mike's association with the Zito family, Gloria also had a very endearing bond with the lady. Inasmuch that one of Mom Zito's eccentricities was that she enjoyed riding around the city on streetcars, with particular emphasis on Gloria being her driver. I'm told the streetcar company sends Mrs Zito a schedule of Gloria's rota every week!"

The reader needs to bear an important factor about the Zito family in mind before becoming overcritical about them and before I continue. Firstly, the family are somewhat over generous to folks who they consider 'valuable' and secondly, to remain 'valuable' it is vital that you savvy the implicit rules of the game. When at such time Mrs Zito has clear ideas about what needs to be done about a particular matter in question, she expects all of the players in her game to give a rapid response to her proposal however formidable though it may seem!

Mrs Zito had closed ears and any form of excuse, lies or rejection, justified or otherwise, and the whole positive outcome of the 'players' longevity could be put at risk. Rocco once disclosed to me that his mom's reasoning was that at some point everyone becomes a tad isolated from the fact that they are not immortal and at that crucial point they are therefore quite easily killable. He said his mom was of the 'old school' and didn't cotton to her advice being shoved aside.

"Now listen all you 'children' and I will explain to you why Mrs Zito Sr requested our company – this particularly affects you and Pi dear Mike!" Mike looked at Pi, Pi looked at Mike and they both looked at me quizzically as I began my homily.

"The first question that Mrs Zito threw at me and Gloria was "are you two lovebirds still living in sin, or have you reproached yourselves and put all that evil wickedness behind you?"

This time I understood every word Mrs Zito was telling us even before Aunt Laura's translation!

"Of course at the possible menace of a precipitously early death, I replied that we are still unmarried and apologised for my tardiness and before I'd hardly finished stumbling over my words she also asked about you and Pi Mike!"

At this point Pi was looking quite bamboozled because as yet she hadn't even met the old bird!

"I was obliged to confess that 'yes' you were also deliberating over the sinning issue. On that point she jumped into the continuing discussion ever so quickly and retorted "The word is out that your Mike is fornicating with an innocent girl who has just lost her father.""

"Don't worry my brother, I assured her on your behalf, that you and Pi were about to do the right thing, but like me the pair of you had been somewhat tardy!"

"To cut a long story short children Mrs Zito had already remedied her question and indeed her answer by procuring for us the wedding suite at the Sheraton Connaught Hotel – by all accounts the head director and the maitre d'hotel were 'close friends' of Rocco and before you ask Mike, it's all buckshee!"

"And so I thanked Mrs Zito and of course Aunt Laura with all the jazzy gushings I could conjure and shook the big guy's hand too. Aunt Laura was almost in tears and declared that the Zito family held us to be very 'valuable' to them. By definition that means we may be asked to fulfil the obligation at some unspecified date, but don't worry, it's not unusual!"

Gloria gave me a wink and a tiny tweak and reminded all and sundry "I am starving, come on children let's eat before we waste away."

As we stepped it out toward the kitchen Mike discreetly pulled me to one side ad said in a hushed voice "Off the record Ricky, me and Pi haven't even had a proper snog yet; off the record eh?"

I put my arm around his neck and gave him an enormous king-sized kiss on the head. "I know you haven't Mike – that's how I know you really love this girl."

So finally in the end everything was working out swell for us all on this November morn at The House on Dundas and Vine and you know I never expected for one moment that it wouldn't!

In case you needed reminding

Some days up ahead may come down empty
but not today
which has been the fullest one we've ever known
The best day yet

I thought you all ought to know that
and at the same time
I wanted to say thank you to you all
for everything that's passed between us today

And I wanted to say sorry to you all as well
Sorry for anything that in your mind
you thought might have inadvertently
missed my dawdling attention.

16

Wise guys do the darndest things!

"This isn't the 1930s. This isn't Al Capone et al. Those days are gone. We are in a new era now. We are not shylocks, pimps or thugs. We are businessmen. We have a good thing going here and we can all make a ton of greenbacks if we're smart. Murder is not smart. If bodies start showing up everywhere it will bring the police and the Feds down upon us — and we don't want that!"

— Rocco Zito

The weddings went off remarkably well. It was a hell of a long day and night and something worth talking about in the years ahead.

It was sure an advantage that Chris was able to journey up from Georgia for the big occasion (Megan and Paul had Poly commitments) otherwise, apart from a couple of streetcar retirees, we were somewhat outnumbered by far! We just couldn't grasp where the rest of the entire army of guests came from — maybe five hundred or so and none of whom we actually knew from Adam!

There was caviar, lobster, Crystal champagne and a bevy of old dames who looked like film noir versions of The Stepford Wives.

Mike's wife, our Pi, looked in every way thoroughly gorgeous and wherever she promenaded and spoke her Western Australian lingo just knocked everyone out. There were two or three zoot suited wise guys who had been seriously eyeing Pi until Mike quite unsympathetically hit them in the head with a polo mallet he had procured from somewhere! Unruffled he asked the security guy "would you mind removing these gentlemen from the floor and taking them outside?" After about 20 minutes these annoying guys came back in and behaved faultlessly in every respect!

My wife, our Gloria, looked so pleased. It was like the whole of her body was smiling. She looked so pretty in her size 12 gothic style gown and her million-dollar sized personality. Gloria didn't usually regard 'occasions' much, which is a pity because she sure had the panache to carry them off!

Where is Chris?

A senior official at the Sheraton Connaught said that Chris and Rocco had been having a long discussion in the lounge bar. He said that he'd caught snippets of the conversation when he was having a brunch break at a nearby table. The substance of the conflab seemed to centre around the nature of good and evil; whether spirits existed and whether the polarity in the universe was harmonious! Strange, I never imagined that Rocco had the depth to broach such subjects! As this official again was walking past their table on his return to duties he said that Chris and Rocco were holding hands and necking and were completely oblivious to their surroundings whatsoever.

It all sounded to me that Chris' middle class American Mason-Dixon Line background and Rocco's Mafia-ness, although such strange bedfellows, nevertheless seemed to come together encouragingly very well!

Several days on and Chris telephoned to say that they were up in 'cottage country' and not to worry – which I am glad she mentioned, because we all were, and are still, worried to similar extents.

The crux of the matter was that Chris and Rocco were severely enamoured or, as we say I England, they were 'potty' for one another.

It was nine-ten and Gloria and Pi were preparing supper snacks for us all. The snow and wind outside swept around The House on Dundas and Vine like a demon, however, why would we care, we had everything that life meant and what's more, we knew it!

She opened the door, eased herself out of the frozen Cheve and made an almighty beeline toward the front door of the house. Wherever Chris went she was accompanied by a sweet smell of jasmine and so I knew that Chris had arrived because of the sudden burst of sweet jasmine coming straight out of the passageway toward us.

Dishevelled and with glittering diamond like snowflakes all over her person, she poked her head around the kitchen door and yelled "Don't you all dare go to bed yet; not until you've heard all about my Rocco." I was turning that thought of 'my Rocco' over and over in my mind?

Meanwhile across the other side of town Rocco was assuring Mrs Zito Snr "she's Jewish mom, but who cares about that?"

Chris recounts her rendezvous

I was on my fourth G&T when this guy walked up to me and starts talking like he's an acquaintance of mine. He said his name was Rocco and he knew all of you at The House on Dundas and Vine.

Rocco : "How the hell are you supposed to know who's who in this ashtray with lights – not one person wants to tell you! So I've started my own system where I say to people like you 'Hi, I'm Rocco Zito, I maybe Cosa Nostra, if maybe you are too, then please tell me!"

So I looked him up and down and asked him straight out whether he was Cosa Nostra or Mafia, or whether he was just 'maybe' and he tells me right back:

Rocco : "Mafia is an expression that the outside world tends to use. I belong to an 'Organisation', not the Mafia. You remember Mario Puzo's book 'The Godfather' and the movie they made from it? Well, it did for our 'Organisation' what silicone does for tits – it made both respective subjects stand out!"

By now he (Rocco) had me smiling all over my face and so in an imprudent sort of way I decided to be canderous right back at him and blurted out "My name's Chris Schuster and my husband was a darned good police officer! Rocco seemed to be somewhat sympathetic, as though he grasped the gravity of what I had just told him at that moment in time.

Rocco : "I like cops. I always think of cops as being the 'good-good' guys and people like me, we're the 'bad-good' guys however, deep down we are all good guys."

"The cops stick to their trade and we stick to ours, that way it all works real well. To be perfectly honest Chris, guys like me couldn't survive without our friends in blue in law enforcement. Let me explain it to you Chris. I wear a $1,500 suit, I'm twenty pounds overweight, but because of my friends in the police, no one ever robs me or kicks me in the balls! You wanna know why? I invoke Sister Marion's rule – no chewing gum or eating candy in class – it's bad for your continuity. That's the reason why I don't do prostitution and drugs – Rocco Zito is strictly legit!"

At that point Chris said they stopped gassing and there was a bitty breathing space in the conversation. It wasn't that our tete-a-tete had become uncomfortable, it was merely a natural break. Not unexpectedly it was Rocco who spoke first.

ROCCO : "Chris, you used the past tense when referring to your husband – would you feel agreeable to recounting what happened – I don't mean to be disrespectful, but I'll tell you mine if you tell me yours?"

I didn't think that there was any big secret about what had happened and so I just came out with it. "He had a heart attack Rocco at just 38 years of age. He had a sudden heart attack whilst playing basketball with our two children! How about you Rocco, are you married?"

For once the bounciness had left his voice. He just looked fixatedly into his empty glass and replied "She was my first steady girlfriend Chris. After some time we got married. I thought I had married the most beautiful girl in the world. We had a kid, he went to the best private school. We lived in a big luxurious house in the nicest neighbourhood in town.

Then I awoke from my oblivious sleep to find that she had gotten 'everything' 'I' had always wanted. Some unkind people remarked that 'I' had gotten 'everything' that 'I' deserved – but what do they know eh?"

Rocco had a lodge in cottage country and we spent the next couple of days shooting the breeze on every side of creation from Houdini to Catholics, Jews and Spiritualism. The days were worth waking up for, and the nights…

I cannot imagine ever being without Rocco, although I am content to take my time. It was as though I was growing again and I desperately needed this somebody, rather than carrying on marking time alone.

The serene upshot of it all was that Rocco felt the same way too!

Dreams run to reality and once or twice the marriage works,
though in the end reality dissolves completely into dream

– Rod McKuen

I7

Polar-ity!

When I'm watching my TV and a man comes on and tells
me how white my shirts can be, but he can't be a man 'cause
he doesn't smoke the same cigarettes as me

— Rolling Stones 'Satisfaction'

Late one Sunday evening toward the furthermost part of Mike's
storytelling session, Gloria made us all a nightcap of hot chocolate with marshmallows and presented us with a platter of fresh-
ly baked brownies straight out of the oven. Mike and Pi took
theirs up to bed with them. Next morning Pi remarked that eating Gloria's brownies was the nearest she ever got to achieving
nirvana – Mike told me that he had indigestion all night! Clearly,
Gloria had added her own 'special' ingredients to the melange!

The entire day before, Mike and Pi spent packing for their
three-day excursion to the Big Apple "for entertainment and ne-
gotiations" Mike said, but wouldn't elucidate any further. "Tell
you when we get back" is all he would say!

Pi cranked up the car radio and found a station playing some
good Christmas rock music. She jiggled in her seat to get comfy
and munched into another of Gloria's brownies. Mike on the
other hand was taking an obligatory ten minutes to warm up the
car's old engine before they cast off proper.

It was quite early in the am and therefore it was still semi-dark – passing our neighbor's houses, each was lit up like primary-colored cupcakes waiting for the holiday season. They entranced Pi. She could see inside some of the houses, even people moving around and 'getting ready for work' she thought. One house had an elaborate Nativity scene in the front garden. Everything was there – Joseph and Mary, Christ and the manger, the hay (albeit covered in snow) and even the three wise men. Pi reached for her camera in the car dashboard, but the traffic lights turned green and Mike drove on.

As they left the city the empty branches of trees could be seen looking distressed and poking sharply into an ominous grey cloud that seemed to stretch for miles and miles. The grey cloud of resentful progress that we all knew was credited to the many factories and landfills in and around the city – so sad!

On that snowy day in late November, Mike and Pi snatched pancakes with jam and maple syrup from a small roadside restaurant – just $1.99 and coffee and it took just a wink and a whistle to make!

By the time they arrived at Mike's brownstone apartment on sixty-eighth street they were plain tuckered out, but after showering and eating the evening was suggesting that a peachy bombshell was about to be unveiled for Pi!

A person cannot hide a major revelation for long, especially from someone who is as perceptive as Pi – as quickly as Mike had begun humming 'Dream Lover' she was way ahead of him.

"Told you I'd take you" he said and added "Put on your glad rags girl, we are going to the Copa!"

Bobby Darin was one of the very few nitery performers who could click with all age groups. Despite his relative youth, he was a real pro with a song delivery and stage presence that was second to none.

When Bobby opened at the Copa the maitre d' was able to provide a stage-side table because of Mike's celebrity status. It was a beautifully candlelit host's table and the only complication was that we would be obliged to share it with Groucho Marx who was 'ringsiding' Bobby's show. Mike told me later that his Pi didn't have a clue who Groucho Marx was and eyed him with some suspicion – she referred to him as 'Sir' or 'Mr Groucho'!

Needless to say the whole show was spectacular in all its elements. Bobby astounded even our Mike. By all accounts when Bobby finished on his upbeat number 'That's All' his jacket was off and collar open.

Years later I recall Mike telling me about Bobby's performance. "The guy had balls-to-the-floor energy, it was just a fucking miracle that he's lived as long as he did!"

It was undoubtedly an evening which Pi would fondly remember and certainly an evening to swank to her university chums about. The pinnacle of the evening being when 'Mr Groucho' formally introduced Pi to Bobby backstage. Mike said he detected in Bobby's demeanour that he liked Pi, and added "better than that Sandra Dee eh?"

After all of the punters had gone their separate ways, and indeed Bobby himself had said his 'toodle-oo's', Mike had sat at the bar for a spell with the maitre d' and the great Groucho Marx (who Mike said seemed to be getting his second wind)!

It had been an exceptionally long day and dear Pi had found herself a comfy chesterfield and was beginning to send the cows home. Mike remarked how Groucho was fascinated by the idea of 'manifestation', whereby dead folk appear in physical form. I knew that Mike had evidence of this abnormally taking place and all that I can add is that I am truly regretful that I wasn't there that evening!

The following day Mike had an interview with (as he described them) "some management lackeys from the Philip Morris Tobacco Corporation."

It all hinged on the fact that since 1954 Mike had been wanting to be 'The Marlboro Man'. Mike's old compadre Christian Haren had grown tired of being The Marlboro Man and Mike saw the opportunity and stepped in fast.

Mike knew that Philip Morris had a bevy of models lined up, but none with his popularity and reputation and also, beyond question, none who owned and drove a Vincent Black Shadow bike!

Mike's whole pitch was for Philip Morris to ditch the outdated cowboy individual and his horse and replace him with a Brando like character with a Vincent Black Shadow motor cycle. I told Mike "it works for me kid!"

Our Mike mesmerized those high-level tobacco lackeys of that I am sure. However, as is often the case, they in turn were obliged to outline Mike's suggestion to the new CEO – "a safe bet that he's still in diapers" Mike ill-humouredly added.

Why is that woman over there buying enough food to withstand a nuclear winter? What is that old fella doing risking a heart attack by trying to wrestle an enormous fir tree into the back of his car? What is the man in a white unkempt beard and a red tunic doing talking to little children? Why will vast business empires grind to a halt and why will traffic jams be a thing of the past? Why were Mike and Pi coming out of Macy's beaming like Cheshire cats and clutching a mountain of parcels and why will there be a sudden predilection for mistletoe at The House on Dundas and Vine? Mike and Pi couldn't wait to get back to Canada and find out the wondrous answers. Their business accomplished in N.Y., tomorrow morning they would be homeward bound.

'Of all the suckers in all the towns in all the world they walk into me'

— adaptation from 'Casablanca'

Mike on their 'run in'

On the far side of 68th street it was like a dense déjà vu had taken over our lives, I wasn't fearful of these unlikely hoodlums harming me or Pi, I was fearful of Pi seeing me harm them!

Same bunch of unforgettable, unfortunates who suddenly appeared out of the woodwork on Dr King day; same little guy with the wonky eye as well.

"I remember you; you dat English wizard guy who took a pigeon out of my buddy's baseball jacket – just like that!"

Mike said "Yes, I is 'dat' guy; now what have you jerks been up to?"

The big guy had been eyeing Pi up and mockingly remarked "Brought your daughter with you today – she a wizard too?"

With an icy smirk across his face Mike replied "Yes, as a matter of fact she is a wizard too – she has the most amazing powers. For example, if you were to touch her you would die the most horrifying death and immediately."

Mike told me afterwards that he remembered wondering if the guy was familiar with double entendres?

The wonky eye fella had been staring at Mike's knuckles. Years ago Mike had had his fingers tattooed after going to see the 1955 movie 'The Night of the Hunter'. Mom gave Mike a hellish beating when he got home, however the damage was done. In fact as Mike progressed in his psychic 'trade' the tattoo helped to solidify his image somewhat.

Mike began to explain the tattoos across the knuckles and fingers of both his hands.

"Ah, little lads, you're staring at my fingers. Would you like me to tell you the story of right hand, left hand? The story of good and evil?

H-A-T-E! It was with this left hand that old brother Cain struck the blow that laid his brother low.

L-O-V-E! You see these fingers dear hearts? These fingers have veins that run straight to the soul of man.

The right hand friends is the hand of love. Now watch and I'll show you the story of life. Those fingers dear hearts are always a-warring and a-tugging, one again t'other. Now watch 'em! Old brother left hand he's a-fighting and it looks like love's a goner. But wait a minute! Hot dog, love's a-winning! Yes sir-ree! It's love that's won and old left-hand hate is down for the count!"

Mike had watched that movie many times since those bad old days and had pretty much memorised word for word said by the evil Reverend Harry Powell character who was played with gusto by the great Robert Mitchum – and finely acted with the same chill, by our Mike.

Mike told me that he knew he had achieved an Oscar nomination for best actor when hardly had he finished his homily the wonky eye guy's mood changed and almost gibberishly he said "Your weird daughter and you freak me out wizard. You, the undead; the son of the son of Frankenstein. We ain't no wicked wrongdoers and don't want no rotating head Vincent Price types knocking us up in the night so you and her fuck off and don't come looking for us again OK?"

And so the day ended well although by all accounts Pi was slightly pissed off by the wonky eye guy frequently referring to her as being Mike's daughter! Said she "I swear if he had said it one more time Mike I'd have kneed him in his goolies!"

Bet 'wonky eye' was pleased he didn't mess with an Australian gal and Mike too eh?

18

It's so amazing about Rocco's Mom!

It's not that often we are all together with absolutely sweet Fanny Adams to do other than eat chocolate and watch TV. However, tonight was kind of a special treat because the thumper bumper Christmas programming had taken its course and they were airing Xmas Andy Williams and Xmas Jacky Gleason back-to-back, followed by 'The Outer Limits'.

In fact, it's fair to say, that we were all glowing with ecstaticness over the recent success of Christina's new relationship with Rocco. Withall that dear girl has been on her own now for years.

It was Pi who first heard a light rapping upon the lounge window pane and when she pulled the drape it was Rocco.

"That man nev-er rest nev-er" says Gloria. "He's day-ting you every single night."

"Oy, Oy, Oy!" Christina joined in "It's my Rocco!"

By now I'd made it to the window and could determine Rocco dragging an immensely large object in a body bag from his new cherry-red Ford Mustang (model 2+2) parked in 'our' driveway!

"I think that Rocco's 'stop by' is more of a cause for concern than a social visit" said Mike hurrying outside to assist Rocco in dragging the object into our garage.

I could tell that Christina was beginning to reconstruct events in her mind by the huge groan she just let out. I gave her a kiss on the forehead and headed out to join Mike and Rocco in the garage.

Gloria, her usual unruffled self, had taken Pi by the hand and I could hear the familiar rattle of cups coming from the kitchen.

Rocco just stood there staring at us, he looked like I'd never seen him look before; uncomfortable and shamefaced! "His name is Joe Donnatelli" he said unhurriedly and then added "I need to dispose of his body!"

Rocco smiled at us both superciliously to signify that he, Rocco, didn't have a clue of what to do!

A rather decisive life and death discussion by somewhat kindred spirits was to follow which I shall disseminate to my reader thus...

MIKE: "With the greatest respect dear Rocco, I had always imagined that the removal and disposal of undesirable folks' bodies was sort of your family forte!"

RICKY: "Me too Rocco; and I reiterate my brother Mike's deepest respect, but even we are aware of the fact that unwanted cadavers usually and traditionally are more than inclined to end up in the tobacco fields and ten to one it's along the Erie course line."

ROCCO: "I agree and that is precisely on the nose the brain teaser that I am unfortunately left with. Like you say guys, *everyone* is aware that the missing cadaver is out there in the fields somewhere – it's common knowledge, even the cops once in a while go out to the fields and just dig up any old remains to save face. However, on this occasion, and no matter how slim the risk is, it's a risk I cannot take. I need new ground; overworked burial tracts like the tobacco fields are totally unsound under these circumstances."

MIKE: "What circumstances are we talking about here Rocco? Who was this guy Donnatelli and why do you hold him in such high regard? Do you want to tell us the reason?"

ROCCO: "On the contrary guys, I do not hold that scum suckling pig Donnatelli in any regard whatsoever. As far as I am concerned he got his just desserts and his executioners are worthy of credit. Ricky, Mike – the guy was a blackhearted paedophile and that's the reason why Mom and Aunt Laura put the kibosh on him. When this guy is gone he has got to remain gone. The possibility of some curious busy body unearthing him at a later date must be zip, nada, diddly-squat!"

RICKY: "Well I'm pleased you came to us about it Rocco. Good relationships are built on trust. You have our assurance, and I'm sure we have yours, to keep everything all-inclusively in the family. So right now let me go talk to Gloria and find out how she figures we ought to deal with the recently deceased Mr Joe Donnatelli!"

About forty minutes later we all of us assembled in the kitchen over beakers of 'overcharged' espresso coffee and Gloria's chocolate cake. We were about to have, which can quite accurately be described as a 'war summit'! Many quality suggestions of how to dispose of the body crossed the table, but it was Pi who finally succumbed to all of the excitement by advocating that we 'plunk' the boring creep into Lake Ontario!

GLORIA: "You remember I took you to Sammy's Garage on Dufferin Street don't you Ricky? Well folks, my old dad used to own the garage and before he passed away he bequeathed the property to me, along with this house – The House on Dundas and Vine. The proviso was that I would allow Sammy to continue doing his motor mechanicing at the garage rent free. Sammy had been dad's chief mechanic and right-hand man for over thirty years."

"Now, here's where I get to the best part and you are all going to like this, especially you Rocco. At the rear of said premises is an old unused dilapidated outbuilding encompassed by rusted skeletons of busted-up vehicles, oil drums and broken triplex glass. In the very midst of this no- man's-land is an 8x2 service pit, inactive since dad serviced Eugene the Jeep during WW2!"

"Don't get ahead of yourselves children, we are only able to access the site during Saturday and Sunday – this is when Sammy visits his beloved daughter who lives in Toronto. It's Thursday today and so tomorrow we need to acquire a large amount of gravel, sand and cement and perhaps some topsoil for cosmetic purposes – does everybody agree?"

And so it was my amazing wife Gloria who saved the day. She had it all figured from start to finish, as though this type of crisis happened all the time!

After the successful implementation of our dastardly deed I was curious to know how Aunt Laura and Mom Zito, both venerable ladies of somewhat advanced years, managed to administer a 'hit' on an individual as street-smart and devious in nature as Donnatelli.

Rocco gave me his best Sicilian smirk. "Elementary Ricky; they used his own smarmy ego. First they went into raptures regarding his radio show, next they invited him to supper and then, whilst Aunt Laura fed him her 'digitalis laced' scones, Mom was able to stick him with her 10" hat pin; right through his black heart – elementary my dear Ricky!"

19

Happy holiday all, especially Megan n Paul!

The chances are that every man jack of us had been Christmas watching since early October and now, as the last handful of days tugged by, there was without doubt a feeling of something magical in the air. A whole series of 'different from what is usual' rituals were hankering to be performed; everything from kissing under the mistletoe, dangling baubles on the Christmas tree to setting light to Gloria's Christmas pudding and yanking Christmas crackers together.

It had been a rare week in which our Christina hadn't hardly gotten off the telephone to Megan and Paul over what they would like to do during the holiday. Unanimously Megan and Paul, and everyone else involved, plumped that they should be staying at The House on Dundas and Vine!

It had previously been suggested that Megan and Paul might be so inclined to spend the holiday with their grandma and grandpa who indubitably would have overindulged them. However, even that sugary proposal crashed. When likened to being introduced to all the new-fangled fine folk at The House on Dundas and Vine there was no contest at all!

20

Megan and Paul's story

For Megan and Paul from small town Georgia, Canada conjured up 'Britishness'. So, with that in mind, and so that they arrived in Toronto with the right credentials, they decided upon stopping over in Atlanta in order to equip themselves with some 'switched on threads'.

Megan was very choosy and hard to please, but finally opted for a showy bell-bottom pants suit and some ironic granny shoes, plus some notably large earrings that would never fit in a jewellery box! Paul on the other hand had his mind set on Beatle boots and a gaudily dyed velvet (or satin) suit.

Toronto was admittedly not swinging London as depicted in Time and Newsweek. The Londoners in American magazines and television reports were a hybrid of comically stereotyped Brits in any event – ineffectual, quaint and slightly befuddled as projected by John, Paul, George and Ringo. The truth was that people in the regions were just as unsophisticated as they had always been – not unlike at all of small provincial towns anywhere in the Western world.

However, that didn't cross the minds of Megan and Paul and why should it, as they boarded the Amtrak and embarked upon perhaps the most long-winded journey of their lives to Toronto – change at Buffalo in 6 and three-quarter hours though!!

Unhurried they comfied themselves and it was Paul who spoke first:

"Our Mom is going to marry a gangster!"

"No she's not!" interjected Megan on the defensive. "A gangster is a hood, a criminal, a crook."

"Okay" says Paul. "She's perhaps goin' to marry a Mafioso!"

"No she's not!" Megan was vexed now. "Rocco is a Sicilian business man, a hotshot, the head of a powerful organisation who make millions of dollars by just influencing folk."

"Yea, like the Cosa Nostra" said Paul, but saves grace by adding "Hell, dear sister I don't really care. When dad was a cop he often said to me "keep in with the rogues and the honest folk won't hurt you."

Megan looked at Paul over the top of her sunglasses. "Yea dear brother, he repeated that statement to me too and having said that you have taken his words out of context. You do realize that he was referring to the police as being the 'rogues'!"

Overcome decisively by his kid sister Paul just replied uneasily "Well it's the darn same thing isn't it?"

21

Why Christmas Eve is so important:
verbosed by Gloria

For the faithful Christmas Eve is the most exciting and holy part of the midwinter festival. Why? Because it heralds the moment, among more fanatical believers, that Christ was born at the very minute of midnight on 25th of December. So when you hear the bells ringing out at the midnight hour it's because Christ is entering the world and the devil is leaving it!

It's Christmas Eve at The House on Dundas and Vine and none of us heathens being of a distinct scriptural persuasion, well we unanimously voted to skip midnight mass! Unfortunately Ricky had to go to work tonight so as an alternative to mass we all agreed to take Ricky by sweet surprise instead. Inasmuch, that at 10pm precisely as Duffy's prepared for the Christmas countdown and Ricky prepared for his last song of the evening we all intended to spew into Duffy's bar.

Zito is owner/proprietor of the establishment and, with that in mind he, urged on by Mike, had cunningly arranged for maitre d' Ernestine De Roche to insist upon Mike singing 'Rudolph the Red-Nosed Reindeer' as a playout number we knew he would hate!

The House on Dundas and Vine

We all had an enthusiastic appetite for late night victuals and so an after hours beanfeast had been organised for all of us and the employees as well once the punters had gone home.

Remember Mindy the hatcheck girl? Well, she was back with her ostrich head husband and couldn't quite get to grips regarding the relationship between all of us at The House on Dundas and Vine. Mike, always one to oblige, explained it to her beautifully in not so many words:-

This is Zito – you know Zito, he's your boss!
He's Christina's fiancé.
This is Christina!
She's Pi's stepmother.
This is Pi!
She's my wife.
I am Mike!
Ricky's younger brother.
This is Ricky!
He's Gloria's husband and Darinesque singer!
This is Gloria!
She's Christina's cousin and also Pi's stepmom.
Not forgetting these handsome youngsters Megan and Paul who are Pi's stepsister and brother and soon to be Zito's step children!!

I recall the look of exhausted frustration on Mindy's phizog, although her husband seemed to follow the connections without difficulty – his name is Don!

22

On the twelfth day of Xmas my true love sent to me . . .

Twelfth Night, the 6th of January 1966. Our Christmas season had undeniably lasted far in advance than we had intended it to. We'd all of us been lollygagging aimlessly like there was no tomorrow for far too long. However, there was no mistaking that officially Xmas had passed and we were hatefully obliged to ridiculously return to tediously mundane worlds – inescapably so.

It was inhumanly raw that Tuesday morning; the type of frigid cold that disintegrates your consciousness. I tried to avoid a glimpse of the row of suitcases in the narrow passageway. They did little to make you feel that some irreparable radioactive dust had sullied us and also our home. Although fallaciously so, The House on Dundas and Vine felt as though it was going to be uninhabited until the end of time as we knew it.

Tears fell, they were utterly shameless tears and for the spunky among us it was undetectable internal sobs – the type that leave your lungs without one drop of air!

Nowhere, never was there more justification and resolve among all of us to create a hybridized family of our very own. To sweep away our furthermost fears and boundaries, throw caution to the wind and accept the privilege of being whole with each other as our benefaction. The evening before we all had pledged to be reunited by late spring – this pledge had become a guarantee!

*A person can succumb of their own free will to too much love
— especially a love that has cogency to enhance reality*

– Ricky Dale

23

A season in the sun

I never imagined for a minute that the day would come when I'd see a Mafiosi shed tears.

"I've just bid farewell to my Christina and her children" he said, wrestling with the fact that he'd not gone with them. "I borrowed Mom's limo and her careful lady driver – they should be in Georgia by suppertime."

He looked at me sheepishly. "I realise that I should have accompanied them on the journey, but honestly Ricky I've got stuff that needs my attention here and now."

There was a loud beep of a vehicle horn outside in our driveway followed by Mom's chauffeur yelling "Get your behind in gear Rocco, your gal needs you!" I walked to the kitchen door and I yelled back "He's coming!" and with it sticking out a mile I added "Looks a lot like you are going to Georgia Rocco!"

Christina eagerly leapt from the limo and wrapped her arms around him as though she hadn't seen him for a week when it must have been all of 30 minutes!

"I know I'm a knucklehead Ricky, but would you mind looking after the 'shop' whilst I'm away? I'll justify my tardiness with Aunt Laura and she'll be sure to put you wise! Don't concern yourself about absenting Duffy's for a while – I'll square it with Ms De Roche too. Hey Ricky! It's like you'll be their boss now!"

I assured dear Rocco by giving him an intense hug and telling him to 'get on his way'. Just to add some panache I replied "No problem Rocco, I'm on it… I ain't eliminating no one though, ok?"

I heard a rumour via the grapevine that there was a seemly alright gal singer doing the rounds in Toronto. Apparently she used to be a singing waitress at El Rancho Diner on Queen Street. She called herself Vicky Vale. Perhaps I'll audition her for Duffy's; although she'd better be to a higher standard and somewhat healthier than her predecessor Ricky Dale!

I could teach her music quickly and without the pain and she could show me how to make a quiche Lorraine[3]

– Cheez Whiz!

---

3   My Gloria adores quiche Lorraine – not the way that I make it though!

24

Mike gets 'lucky'!

When a person is told "You're so New York!" what in heavens name does that plainly ambiguous remark mean? Is it a compliment or a criticism? Mike's long-time dear compadre Christian Harren said it to Mike this afternoon and Mike, bless him, was still trying to figure the complexed expression out!

"Perhaps I may never know." He chewed it over. "Perhaps it's merely some kind of hackneyed phrase and no one actually really knows what it does mean."

"Colder than a witch's tit in a cast-iron bra" was yet another saying that didn't make much sense. Mike couldn't recall where or when that saying had come from or indeed who had said it. However, what he did recall was that the weird expression always came into his head when it was snowing like hell and yet the sun was still shining. Precisely the way it was doing that unpleasant afternoon in New York.

Christian and Mike had arranged to meet up for coffee and a greasy slice of Rays Pizza in Little Italy early in the p.m. Mike had had a second formal meeting with the Philip Morris Board and Christian was anxious to hear the outcome.

Christian Harren had been Philip Morris' Marlboro Man for years, but had grown tired of it. Christian tipped Mike off that Morris could be looking for a replacement, however Philip Morris had made up their minds to defunct the whole concept of the 'Marlboro Man' for the time being.

"Sorry I wasted your time Mike. I guess it wasn't to be and I don't want to send you on another ineffectual mission. However, I've heard that Luckies are planning an extensive promotion taking up space on at least three radio stations. Needless to say Mike hadn't heard about this new venture by Luckies and said he would be following it up "this very p.m."

Christian gave Mike a huge dogged smile. "You're just so New York, my Mike". He planted a smacker on Mike's forehead and went on his way.

That evening on the telephone Mike couldn't wait to tell Pi the news. In fact we were all sat around the telephone and Pi was kind of relaying to Gloria and I and writing notes on her scratch pad as well!

In essence, the American Tobacco Co. had put Mike on their payroll to be their 'Celebrity Smoker of the Month'. It was all going to be pre-recorded with Mike lecturing the great American public on what makes Luckies so good! All of that inter-balanced with dumb-ass phrases and jingles.

Mike thought that the whole incomprehensible plan relied upon people's insanity! Here's a snippet that springs to mind:-

"Light a Lucky when you are tempted to eat between meals – they satisfy that silly craving for sweets and rich pastries. That's why thousands are now reducing (dieting) and smoking Luckies constantly. And don't forget Lucky Strike are toasted!"

Mike did give the thumbs up to one ad though:-

"Lucky separates the men from the boys, but not from the girls."

It seems to me that whilst commercially campaigning for Luckies, Mike was also putting his name in the public eye which cannot be a bad thing at all. So all's well that ends well eh – LSMFT![4]

---

4   Lucky Strike means fine tobacco

25

Spoken by Pi, thus:—

We don't have iced days in Queensland or anywhere in the southern hemisphere for that matter. What we do have though in super abundance are ice cubes in cherry soda, coke and almost nearly every intoxicating spirit.

When Mike and I went to Manhattan he took me to an outside skating rink in Central Park – it was only the first occasion that I'd actually walked on ice! I slipped my hand into Mike's hand, wearing puffy gloves, and I kind of used him for balance. I really wanted to show off to Mike by doing figure eights, skirt twirling, ponytail swirling like the other girls on the rink, but all I could manage was one skate at a time.

Mike chanted alongside me "One, two, three, push! One, two, three, push!" I tried to follow his voice, but was obliged to whisper "Shhhh Mike! You're embarrassing me." He stopped chanting immediately and gave me a whopping hug which picked me up off my feet!

When two persons fade into one another by locking lips and hugging, that's pure joy. It was all I could ruminate about as I made my way to McMasters on that staggeringly wintry morning after Xmas semester.

Contemplative thoughts about my Mike, my husband, were not the only thing on my mind. The nearer I got to the university building the more I was beginning to get into an unimaginable, nay unwarranted, flap over my white gold wedding and diamond cluster engagement rings! As I promenaded up the driveway to the hallways it was as though my ring finger had become an item of prominence. Like it was sticking out and eye-catchingly saying "Look at me!"

So silly of me really because when I reached my tutorial group it was as if I had become a famous person, but everyone was patting me on the back and congratulating me – it was so lovely! Seemingly the cat had been let out of the bag a week or more before, after the Hamilton Spectator had zoomed in on the wedding reception at the Sheraton Connaught.

I managed to retrieve a copy of the Spectator to show everyone at The House on Dundas and Vine. It was a massive news story which contained a middle page pull-out, if you were so inclined. The reason it was an exceptionally brilliant scoop was mainly because many of the 500 plus guests were a 'complex structure' of influential 'families' in southern Ontario!

January, come down easy please!

When the first flake falls on Hamilton, Ontario
The whole city is given to pretending it's the first snowflake ever.
Therein lies the clue…
Like a half-forgotten joke
Surprises, like snowflakes
Lose their original excitement and awe
When relived or retold about.

– Pi Edwards Dale

26

Girl talk – Christina to Megan

I collected my mail yesterday and among boring tabs was a welcome letter from our Gloria. She asked how Zito was settling in and also offered me some quite helpful guidance.

With regard to my Zito, I wrote back and told her how he had really transformed from a 'good' to 'better' guy! Inasmuch that he had never done any type of blue-collar job in his life so it was really weird seeing him with paint brush in hand. What was even more weird was the fact that he was finding painting so enjoyable! So far he had given our bedroom two new coats of paint and skilfully undertaken too! Today he was beginning to sandpaper down the front porch!

I wrote back to Gloria right away because it is important that she cottons on to what a lovely man my Zito is. He is not capable of meanness and all the reports to the contrary are not only untruthful, but probably instigated by Zito's adversaries!

I explained to Gloria that it wasn't purposefully a question of whether Zito's lover (me) was mindfully whitewashing Zito's character and that in many respects Zito was similar to our Mike. He is out-and-out misconceived by folks for the someone who he isn't!

It was the last part of Gloria's letter that really hooked me in Megan. She wrote that when Zito was in his mid-teens he abruptly discovered he'd been born out of wedlock and no matter how medicinal the medicine of his ongoing success was, and how comforting it was to know how really loved he was by his mother, the fact was that there was still that gap of who his father was!

Although his first marriage was a big mistake – they were both far too young. He gives great importance to the genuine devotion felt by him and his new Georgia family.

And so please preserve that thought Megan and tell me how you and Paul might react in the event that I were to ask you both to discreetly get into your car, drive into town and go see either the Justice of the Peace for Gwinnett community, or the Clerk at the County courthouse all for the purpose of booking a non-religious marriage ceremony real soon – s'il vous plait!

How many times
Have I been asked
Or asked to define love

What can it mean?

Your love for your children
Is one definition
Good music
May be one too.

Baseball
Hockey
Ice Cream
Peanut Butter
And my Zito
Is one too.

– Christina, March 1966

27

"He spoke with his gat, rat-a-tat-tat!"

With Mike away in NY and Christina and Rocco away in Georgia we spent our time just attending to business and earning a buck. Gloria patiently ferrying the population of Hamilton to and fro; Pi snowed under with academic challenges and me putting pen to paper and making out I can write!

During the evening times Pi could be found sitting at the kitchen table doing studenty things and Gloria would be tidying The House on Dundas and Vine before taking a leisurely shower. Once in a while I'd put my pen and paper down and snatch a tender kiss with Gloria under the shower – sometimes just a little more if she felt so inclined.

This particular evening was the evening before I was due to commence 'minding the shop' for Rocco whilst he was away. It seemed like a good idea to call him just to confirm details and of course to let him know that I hadn't forgotten! And there was a couple of 'nuisance' dilemmas that I wanted to straighten out with him as well. I guess that I could have written him a letter, but I often found that a telephone call was not so 'restricted' as was putting everything on paper.

For me, him being my 'boss' was a serious matter and so with that thought I took the initiative and plunged in first.

"Rocco my dear friend, as I'm shortly going to become your principal right-hand man, your eyes and ears, don't you agree that perhaps I ought to adopt a somewhat different persona to my existing one? Inasmuch the first thing that springs to mind is that I should refashion my name to a name that is more distinct and in keeping with the tough-nut that I am supposed to be posing as."

The telephone went quiet for a second or two and then it was Rocco who spoke. "What sort of pro tem name did you have in mind dear Ricky?" I was pleased that Rocco was at least entertaining the change of name suggestion and so I encouragingly replied "It seems to me Rocco that the 'Ricky Dale' moniker is a depiction of a soppy insignificant crooner which, although that is in fact what I am, it is not a suitable name for a head honcho. For instance, a name such as 'Rocky McCarthy' gives more of an impression of an individual that folks would want to avoid upsetting!"

"Withall to all intents and purposes I am seemingly going to be your 'Frank Nitti'. A big shot, an enforcer if necessary."

I heard Rocco quietly chuckle as he replied. "Hey Ricky, if you are Nitti, that makes me a scar-faced Al Capone, complete with syphilis... not too certain that I like that image my lovely friend! I know that you mean well Ricky, but perhaps you've watched one too many episodes of the 'Untouchables'. Hell Ricky, why don't you call yourself 'Greasy Thumb Guzik'? He was indeed a Capone lieutenant too!"

"Don't you worry my dear friend. Just be yourself and I give you my word that my guy Robski will never stop watching your back. I don't want you feeling like a sitting duck in a shooting gallery and let me assure you that there are very few professional 'gunsels' still in the market place for work these days. I'll be certain to message Eliot Ness and the Bureau regarding your concerns though!" he added cheerfully.

Later that evening I ran my ideas and my conversation with Rocco past Gloria. She is a person with great intuition and perceptiveness in such matters.

"Although paperwork has always bored and irritated me Gloria, nevertheless I am committed to making certain that this 'babysitting' venture for Rocco is a complete commercial/financial success for him and indeed an individual personal achievement for me as well."

"I am going to rid this organisation of any bad apples and absolutely ensure that invoices are issued for every transaction. I am also going to put in place a monthly stock take. I cannot believe that a crate of whisky can just disappear; at least that's what he told me. There are going to be a lot of people with red knuckles once RD takes the reins! I completely agree with Rocco; it's not necessary to hypothetically slick down my hair with brilliantine and clean my fingernails with a stiletto to become a revered boss. Nevertheless, it is likely that I shall make definite improvements to the slapdash present system."

I hadn't stopped talking and my dear Gloria was not impressed, even one iota with anything I'd said! "No, no, no Ricky Dale! You are going to get yourself mowed down real quick and maybe me also! You really must close a blind eye. Do not be a Clarence Darrow. Please let those sleeping dogs lie; unless you don't mind checking under your vehicle hood each and every day before you touch the starter!!

Wish that I were Bogey

San Quentin, Sing Sing, Alcatraz
He busted out of them
Like no one ever has

The smoke he blew, at you
Lip curled so nastily too
Flared nose and narrowing eyes
Revered, his first disguise

Robinson, Cagney and Raft
Were never any match
He'd whistle down Bacall
And Hepburn was an easy catch

I adored the everything he did
Especially clinking Ilsa's wine
"Here's looking at you kid"
Wish that I were Bogey every time!

– Ricky Dale, March 1966

28

Seance on a February morning

The long winter days passed slowly and methodically by, almost flowing into one another like the movements in a synchronized symphony. We were thankful that at least those cutting January winds had turbulently blown themselves out. I guess that it's so easy for each of us to put the blame upon the seasons, although to be perfectly candid this winter of '66 had to be the most ungentle I had ever known.

Mrs Zito looked every bit the cat's pyjamas wrapped up in her long shawl. There was something luxurious-de-lux about her that made you feel like you ought to bow to her in a queenly manner. She had been joined this morning by her guardian par excellence by the name of Robski Drakulic, dressed head to toe in furs. The two of them were surely a contrast to the dozen or so other passengers on Gloria's bus who looked decidedly dull.

Robski enjoyed working for the Zito family, perhaps because in many respects they were 'old school' folks, somewhat similar to him.

Robski Drakulic was indeed a man who realized his place in life. He was the child of a communist Yugoslav army officer and so in that regard everything was perfectly clear to him from the start. God did not exist; religion is the opium of the masses and churches per se are nothing more than monuments of history and culture!

Gloria often behaved as though she had proprietorship of the bus company. Indeed there were many individuals who truly believed she did. Her first port of call that ominous morning was the recently launched Tim Hortons on Ottawa Street. "Any of you guys want to buy some delicious donuts?" she hollered down the gangway of the bus. It was obvious that many passengers shared her partiality for hot donuts by the string of folks following her out into the cold. Gloria was of course aware that she was taking liberties with the chief executives well timed bus, but gees, it only knocked off two or three minutes out of a whole day!

There were certain passengers who rode her bus every day. Like the bible thumping preacher who always embarked at Birch Avenue and stepped off at St Josephs Hospital. It was amusing to count how many 'Hail Marys' he could squeeze in between the two stops. He was harmless though. I think St Josephs let him out once in a while and he'd return himself to the 'corral' once he'd had enough of the 'villainous' world.

Gloria's bus was now near full as it approached the part of the city named 'Hamilton's Mountain'. I feel a need to explain to my reader that 'Hamilton's Mountain' is not a mountain as such, although the topography does have a rise in elevation of approximately 200 feet.

Gloria knew that Mom Zito would be sitting back and enjoying this part of her excursion – she particularly seemed to get a kick when Gloria picked up speed and the needle was flatlining now at 35 mph!

It was at the junction to the closed down drive-in cinema when all hell seemed to have herald-in. First Gloria heard the distinctive sound of glass being haphazardly punctured and almost in the same breath passengers were on their feet yelling

"It's the sniper, it's the sniper!" at the top of their voices.

She had instinctively brought the bus to a standstill and was halfway back in the bus inspecting the damage. Fortunately not a soul was hurt in the chaos and confusion, however, there were shards and fragments of broken triplex covering the unoccupied seats adjoining Mrs Zito's and Robski's seat.

The crass authorities were clued-up about the sniper difficulty long before he practised his art on Gloria's bus, but by all accounts they didn't think he posed a real threat because no one had been as yet injured or killed! His arrest and detention were not given priority as such. He was considered more of an irritating nuisance risk, that's all!

Whilst all of the flummoxing fracas was being resolved, Gloria hadn't noticed that Robski had decamped the bus by the emergency exit. Mom Zito noticed that Gloria had noticed Robski gone and immediately beckoned Gloria, indicating that she wanted to whisper something of importance into Gloria's ear. "Drakulic made out the trajectory of the shots and juxtaposed them with the situ of the shooter. He won't be gone long. He's gone to chastise the creep!"

Gloria gave Mom Zito a knowing wink and sauntered back to her driver's seat. She sat there serenely just making an effort to process in her mind everything that had developed and then standing and facing the passengers she raised her voice and said "Everything is ok folks, we'll be on our way just as soon as one of our passengers returns from taking a whiz!"

On the subsequent return journey as we were passing Gage Park on our way to the depot, Robski sidled-up to Gloria and murmured "I'll meet Ricky at The House on Dundas and Vine at nine. We'll throw the body into the Niagara River. Tell him don't flap, the evidence is well hidden for now!"

Gloria smiled and mused "Normal procedure I guess!"

(the physical trajectory, together with the damage caused to the interlayer of plastic in the glass, held clues to the shooter's location. That and the fact that the drive-in cinema is the highest point to shoot from.)

Author's admit…

At the risk of blighting an entire chapter, the Hamilton sniper incident differed a shade from the author's interpretation of events.

Here are the unelaborated facts:

Whilst travelling on a bus in Hamilton's Mountain district there was suddenly an almighty bang as the glass in the adjacent window to mine shattered. I later found out that the 'projectile' had embedded itself in some baggage on the luggage rack.

What absolutely astounded me was the nonchalant reaction from the two elderly ladies sat only a few feet away. Quote/un-quote "Aw, it's the sniper again!" In fact, the driver of the bus seemed wholly unconcerned as well as though this occurrence was just an everyday happening!

I didn't get any sympathy from the guys in the band – one of whom remarked "It's obvious to me Ricky that the sniper must have watched your performance yesterday evening!"

29

All in a day's work!

The Niagara River is a breathtakingly awesome sight to behold. A likely explanation for my rapturous thoughts could be that I'd never seen it so up close and personal before! I've resided in the Niagara region for many happy years and visited the falls on numerous occasions and yet I've never once taken a trip on The Maid of the Mist – I don't imagine that I ever will now!

Although Robski and I had gotten somewhat 'windswept' in our appearance due to our untypical escapades in the sticks, we nevertheless agreed to make an early start and head off to Montreal that evening instead of the following morning as originally planned. I telephoned my Gloria to let her know about our change of plan in case she might be concerned that I'd fallen in the river. Off we set, Robski and I, on the next stage of our schedule.

The purpose of our round trip to Montreal was to make ad hoc calls upon the Zito Family business consortiums in order to ascertain their profiteering and such.

Robski insisted that he drove. He wasn't a big talker which suited me as I managed to catnap a bit. Robski, I discovered, was an opera connoisseur, specifically Maria Callas. I must have listened to 'O mio babbino caro' and 'Con onor muore' a dozen times during our Montreal excursion! I kind of liked Callas myself, but now her voice has an association for me with the

Niagara River at midnight!

Robski had us holed-up at his brother-in-law's home on Rue St-Antoine. Him, his wife and kids were really nice regular folk and made me very welcome. He worked as a glazier for a local glass company. Strange coincidence, I could have presented him with a glass replacement job just yesterday – to a bus!

Our first port of call was a cocktail lounge owned by the Zito Family on Rue St-Denis. I really did have the overwhelming desire to just 'okay' their profit and loss accounts and, to be quite truthful, my numerical proficiency sucked in any event. However, with Robski hovering close at hand it seemed sensible for me to at least go through the motions of being meticulous. I guess that what disturbed me the most was the thought that some hapless man or Girl Friday might take the flak for me leaving school at 14 years of age! An even worse and more serious scenario was that they wind-up in the Niagara River because of my tardiness.

With all of that stuff beating me up I got my mojo working and my running total running, crossed my fingers and hoped for the best!

We called upon a couple more franchises after lunch and by the end of the day I was beginning to feel just like a 'pukka' accountant!

It occurs to me that at this juncture my reader may wish to be enlightened regarding the Zito Family affiliations; perhaps some historical background too wouldn't go amiss? I will elucidate as far as I am able.

Montreal had been a favourite gateway for shifting heroin for years because of its close accessibility to the United States border. It had a large Italian immigrant population, plus being part of the French-speaking province of Quebec it was also a natural 'home-from-home' for French and Corsican criminals from Marseilles.

The city also had its own Mafia family led by Vincenzo Cotroni which was allied to the Bonanno family in New York. However, in 1961 the ring was broken open by the RCMP and other agencies and so another point of entry had to be found. It was found in Miami where Meyer Lansky, supposedly retired, took up the reins again.

By now the Montreal connection had settled down and it was around this time that the Zito Family began to surface. It was an opportune moment for them, inasmuch that they were uninterested in narcotics and for that reason they had no intention of treading upon other bosses toes.

The Zito Family described themselves as being exclusively 'business agents' for a Sicilian syndicate; collectively and more commonly referred to as the 'Ndrangheta'. They hailed from Calabria (in the Italian 'toe') and had no allegiances to anyone but themselves.

To the other bosses who were primarily involved in the heroin business, the Zito Family were never considered as any business obstacle whatsoever. Indeed, the recent wedding party given by the Zito Family had included guest invitations to some of the most prominent and influential 'Families' in North America. Opulent suites and extravagant security were provided for all without a single lira cost to the guests!

The following morning Robski and I headed home. He insisted on driving of course, however I'd already decided that I wasn't listening to Callas all the way back and so I had purchased a Tony Bennett tape. Robski seemed to approve – he was humming along to it!

The upshot of our 'fact finding' expedition had a favourable outcome regardless of my scepticism and not a single person got hurt!

It seemed likely that Robski and I may have bonded slightly during the course of the last several days together. I think that the watchwords that govern his behaviour are silence, remoteness and loyalty. He is clearly one of the last remaining old-style 'street soldiers' and that observation kind of saddens me!

30

Ask Robski!

The following day Aunt Laura scheduled Robski and I to visit one of the Zito Family recently acquired business associates. The guy ran a haulage outfit in Scarborough, Ontario which was a suburb just outside of the metropolis of Toronto. By all account the Family had learned that the guy had become somewhat greedy and so it became our job to show him the error of his ways!

The 90-minute drive to Scarborough was perfect because it gave me the opportunity to broach a personal matter with my now new pal Robski.

It involved a rather serious obstacle that my younger brother Mike was trying to find a solution to in New York where he lived and worked. From the beginning I made it perfectly clear to Robski that, under different circumstances, I would have most probably run Mike's sticky situation past Rocco in order that he may come up with a solution, however, on this occasion I was determined to not interrupt Rocco's newly acquired 'exuberance' he had for life. Along with his new wife Christina and their family, not to forget his passion for painting and gardening, Rocco had simply 'transcended'.

'God works in mysterious ways' and for whatever reason a religious zealot had hitched himself to Mike. The guy worked as a freelance reporter and it was in that regard that he had been digging deep and cornered Mike on a whole bunch of stuff best forgotten.

Not only does the guy want to expose Mike as a 'depraved demonologist', but also intended to reveal elements of Mike's life in England when Mike was just 17 years of age!

Robski gave me a short, perplexed look. "So what did Mike get up to in England that was so bad?"

I hesitated and replied "Mike was a blue movie star; jolly good at his job too!"

Somewhat astonished, Robski retorted "What, your Mike did porn?"

"He certainly did" I replied. "It was all done in the best possible taste though!"

"I've never watched a porn movie" Robski confessed. "Do they contain a storyline or is it all just overindulgent shagging?"

"Yea, there often is a storyline – 'Death of a Salesman' it ain't though" I laughed. "It's usually the same storyline each time and of course it culminates with lots of random shagging".

I felt that I needed to come to Mike's rescue and so I built on what I had previously said by adding "The movies that our Mike 'studded' in were very upmarket in the way they portrayed stuff – almost avant-garde! They were not necessarily shot with your second-rate perv in mind."

Robski looked a tad mused "I don't understand Ricky – ultimately shaggin' is shaggin' isn't it?"

"Let me give you an example" says I. "A kind of classy movie that Mike starred in was shot on a houseboat on the River Thames where the occupants were having a rave-up. Mike's the hero who resuscitates a supposedly drunken girl who had fallen overboard..."

"The movie I enjoyed the most was actually shot in a genuine garage in Hackney, East London. The father and son motor mechanics had agreed to allow the film company to use their garage providing they and a few mates could watch the shoot! The plot of the movie was that Mike, supposedly a motor mechanic, was servicing a girl's vehicle when he spills oil on her dress…"

"Mike was so begrimed after the shoot that he drove 300 miles to where I lived in Devon so's he could have a nice hot bath and a change of clothes!" – (he arrived unannounced at 2am! That's my Mike and I love 'im!)

"Around that sort of time-line Mike was also having a fling with an adult model from Texas, name of Candy Barr. Candy was over here in the UK to gain some brownie points in Europe. This newspaper goon knows all about Mike's hanky-panky with Candy too! It all happened a long time ago and Mike is trying hard to carve out a new and respectable life for himself now. What bothers me is not the fact of Mike's involvement in dodgy movies, it's the reality that Pi could find out. I sure as hell wouldn't want that to happen and of course neither would our Mike!"

"Mike tells me that he's tried offering the guy cash and the fella just laughed out loud at him and referred to Mike's money as 'fornication riches'. Says he will bestow his forgiveness and exonerate Mike's past only after Mike has been on air and denounced Satan. The alternative is to say nothing and allow this freak the excuse to amply nail Mike to a Jesus cross in the guy's newspaper expose. We know that this guy is more than likely on some sort of crusade which to all intents and purposes is going to promote his own career, however, if the American Tobacco Co get wind Mike will be history and maybe even looking at a lawsuit for reckless endangerment to their product."

After bending Robski's ear for the past 25 minutes I finally paused long enough for him to ask me "Do you want me to yank the guy's appendix out; what did you have in mind Ricky?"

"Thank you for listening Robski. I would just like you to speak to the guy, perhaps appeal to his better nature and if that doesn't work perhaps 'spook' him a bit – big fella like you, he might find daunting and lose his resolve!"

Robski gave me a fair-minded smile and replied "Yea, he might Ricky!"

31

Happy conclusions

The haulage guy, Guiliano, was without question totally on the level regarding his accounts. Rumours to the contrary were merely tittle-tattle. Be that as it may, he was kind of short-sighted to the fact that his sprightly trophy wife and her sit-upon derriere were malfunctioning beyond repair!

In this type of husband-and-wife scenario, the lifestyle of the saps and indeed the whole lie of the land is a most important factor. Indeed, it is consequential to the delinquency of the couple and the outcome to that delinquency.

You may want to ask yourself – can it be rightful and appropriate to chastise and punish two children when it is only one of those children who has scolded the cat?

In the event that only one child has by design wilfully degraded the trust of its superiors, is it fair that this default should also be the liability of the non-offending child? Surely not!

This notion seems to be pretty much the rationality in which the Zito Family rule. Especially in cases of impropriety by their personnel. However, it is for Robski to decide how he wishes to interpret the rules. In this respect I discovered Robski to be somewhat predictable. Inasmuch that he employs his same unique maxim on every occasion. Guiliano et al were not an uncommon case.

Robski tended to pick out and apply three choices and allow the individuals to opt for which one they preferred. There was never any room for discussion, haggling, powwows or trade-offs. Once the individuals had decided, Robski would conclude the meeting and unfussily leave the room.

In the case of Guiliano and that of his grabby spouse the choices were relatively straightforward:

1 Ditch wife; reimburse Zito Family; continue your business
2 Reimburse Zito Family
3 None of the above!

Robski didn't confide the outcome and I didn't ask!

Based on the assumption that Robski would get back to me in due course I didn't hassle him in regard to a solution of our Mike's profanity imputation. That was why I was to some extent taken aback when he casually enlightened me that the 'Mike problem' had been solved.

It was a couple of days after we had visited Guiliano and this time we were on our way to give another wake-up call to a bookmaker in Burlington, Ontario. I decided to ask Robski how it went.

"Did you have any difficulty convincing the reporter guy?" I asked.

"No difficulty" Robski reported.

"I feel that perhaps I should tell the guy that his decision was appreciated" I added.

"You can't" Robski replied.

"Why?" I asked.

"He's in the Hudson" Robski retorted.

Robski merely added one short sentence. "It was for Pi – Ethan Edwards was my Commanding Officer!"

Robski and I never spoke of it again!

32

April 4, 1968

It seems to me like it's a lifetime ago when my brother Mike and I stood transfixed in awe and watched Dr King deliver his enthralling 'I Have a Dream' speech on the steps of the Lincoln Memorial. It was the balmy summer of 1963 and looking back over the years so much had changed; both personally and politically during the interim.

I like to imagine that the years had turned both Mike and I into responsible 'grown-ups' – although like optimistic adolescents we never lost the belief of there being light at the end of the darkest tunnel. That was before I digested the news headlines; broke ranks and cried like a baby – I expect my Mike did too.

The story was plastered over every newspaper and tv screen in the country – it was like there was no place to hide!

"Dr King is assassinated by a sniper as he stands talking on the balcony of his second-floor room at the Lorraine Motel in Memphis…"

Although I realise that after my initial shock there was bound to be a backlash to my emotion, what I didn't realise was the denial mode that I went into – to a lesser extent I still am in that mode.

April 5

Waking this morning with the warmth and softness of my Gloria right here beside me is undoubtedly the finest way to experience eternity and then rising and gazing out of my window across the soothing landscape of warm haziness is in itself inspiring. It is mornings like this that remind me of what a feeling of 'place' The House on Dundas and Vine gives us – it kind of builds a power within us against wicked and evil. This house and land belongs to us, and we to it also.

Canada can be an empty place in Winter, but in the Spring, Summer and Fall it is filled with wonders that insist upon speaking to you all at once! The Spring begins with a colloquy filled with exquisitely magnificent harvests of color. Hidden and asleep under the snow for months she suddenly awakes and offers up her beauty once again.

Before you know it Summer has teamed up with Spring and all sense of the wild Winter is lost. The meadows become green and gracious again and everywhere bright hues of clustered flowers arrive, each bringing their intoxication of divine color.

The soft yellow buffalo bean; pink and white sun-bleached roses; the gaudy orange and red tiger-lily. Ours to have and to hold.

It has been said that 'beauty' is whatever makes the adrenalin run and Canada's 'garden' is no exception. A 'garden' in a long-settled land, cultivated with love for centuries by the very good and the very wise…or so it seems!

The lenses of Gloria's gold-rimmed glasses seemed to gleam when I mentioned shopping and that I was taking the day off to accompany her on her pre-arranged excursion to Toronto.

When a person initially presumes that they will be shopping on their own and then out of the blue a special someone tags along to keep them company – it's a nicety; wouldn't you agree?

Going on the assumption that anything was possible, I figured that my Gloria had an extra-sensory perception. It's particularly geared toward knowing exactly what's going on in my mind. My point is that, based upon that assumption, she would obviously realise my obsession for wanting to snug-up and have loves early in the a.m., specifically for a spell this morning! Not so brilliantly complexed really.

Folks say to be careful what you wear because Spring can be quite unpredictable, however as we headed out on the 403 highway to Toronto, Winter had all but vanished. I neglected to touch upon the reasons for our Torontonian fun trip. Firstly, Gloria wanted to stop-off and say 'hi' to her fond college buddy Sun Yee Loo. Sun Yee lived on Dundas Street West in Chinatown so it wasn't really out of our way. She was the owner of a small elegant restaurant serving Chinese seafood dishes and tasty vegan cuisine as well.

Above Sun Yee's restaurant the Loo family rented out about 12 reasonably priced rooms which were popular with the University fraternity close by.

Our main port of call was to be Eatons Department Store where I intended to buy some nice things for my Gloria. Although of course the choice would be hers, I nevertheless had in mind an insulated raincoat for the Fall, a whimsical umbrella and perhaps some showy shoes? Eatons also had an excellent perfume bar!

We arrived at Sun Yee's in perfect time for brunch. Gloria must have mentioned that I was going to be coming along with her because Sun Yee kindly presented me with a little book of 'Chinese Verse Translations'. I appreciated this very much and it is probably true to say that until then I had only ever head of 'Confucian' stuff and the like.

There was one verse translation in particular that I was attracted to. It had a sort of 'Canada' ring about it and a really poetic quality as well:-

To escape from thoughts of love;
I put on my fur-cloak
And ran out from the lamp-lit silent house.

On a tiny footpath
The bright moon peeps;
And the withered twigs on the snow-clad earth
Across and across, everywhere scrawl 'Love'.

It was shortly before 11am when Sun Yee excused herself and headed out to the kitchen in order to prepare our brunch. The restaurant was at its emptiest when I saw this thick-set fella with an angry look on his face amble across the dining area. He kind of looked out of place in Sun Yee's establishment; didn't strike me as a connoisseur of fine Chinese victuals at all. As a matter of fact, I remember thinking that a plate of pig's trotters would be more his style. I guess I am intolerant of folks who show no respect when eating out in a decent place such as Sun Yee's, inasmuch that he looked raggedy and ill-groomed. I was also opposed to the redneck duds he was wearing! I subsequently learned that he had rented out one of the Loo family rooms upstairs.

I lit a Lucky for my Gloria and I; we both enjoyed a smoke before eating as it sort of augmented our appetite.

Although I tried not to pay any heed, I was very conscious that the mangy fella was oftentimes smirking in our direction; not one hundred per cent at me, but smugly and unmistakably at my Gloria!

It was a one-time occasion when I chose to forget who I now was, or rather who I had once been, before beginning this new life here in Canada.

Completely out of the blue and with somewhat furious anger I became the arrogant upstart of the kid I had once been over a decade ago in England:

Dramatic drainpipe trousers, winkle pickers shined to perfection, Tony Curtis hair with DA – I'm the bee's knees and nobody get in my way!

Sun Yee's elegant restaurant had become an Espresso bar on the Waterfront – I just put a shilling in the jukebox when I catch sight of some geezer eyeing-up my bird:-

TEEN RICKY – "Hey mush, you oglin' my bird?"

REDNECK – "I'm allowed to look aren't I?"

TEEN RICKY – (quite loud) "No you f…'in ain't Yank!"

REDNECK – "Why ain't I allowed to look?"

TEEN RICKY – "Because I don't like what you're thinkin' when you're looking."

REDNECK – "Hell man, is it a crime in here to think?"

I guess that I did sort of agree that the redneck fella had a point of view that wasn't worth knocking his block off over. With that in mind I figured I'd shut up! He'd now moved his eyes to the delicious victuals Sun Yee had just served him up in any event.

Be all that as it may, my central reason for keeping the lid on things was because it put an end to Gloria pinching my leg!

April 5 had without doubt been a day in the diary of life that would become impossible to forget; more so than we could have imagined at the time.

It had been a significantly productive day for us too; inasmuch that Gloria managed to find all the items she wanted in Eatons. They weren't the items that I had originally pencilled in for her, but what do I know anyways? Apart from being presented with a fine book from Sun Yee, Gloria surprised me too with a black silk stage shirt and dicky bow.

Heading back home on the 403 we stopped and kissed for a spell and I gave Gloria a voluminous bottle of her favourite perfume – I got that one right didn't I!

We arrived back at The House on Dundas and Vine quite late. I could hear Pi on the telephone. I think Mike and her were having a heart-to-heart over Dr King's murder. Perhaps I had been somewhat clumsy – out enjoying life today when so many folks were mourning. I remember a line in which Dr King wrote *"I think the greatest victory we have is something internal."*

I am sure he would have understood why we found it necessary to briefly break away today, rather than bow to grief.

Several weeks had passed by when early one morning we received a telephone call from that nice Sun Yee. It was regarding the redneck guy whose nose 'Teen Ricky' envisaged flattening. Hindsight is too peculiar for this simple writer to contemplate upon. Most probably a million or so Torontonians would agree with my reasoning. The reason being was that our 'nemesis', namely James Earl Ray, had peacefully lived among them for over one month. Unfortunately by the time the RCMP had begun combing the city, Ray had flown off to London, England!

It had taken only 70 minutes for the Dallas police to round up Lee Harvey Oswald; and yet 48 hours after firing the fatal shot at the Lorraine Motel in Memphis, James Earl Ray was disembarking at Toronto's Union Station!

June 5 – footnote:

Presidential candidate Senator Robert Kennedy was shot in a Los Angeles hotel. He died the next day. The killer was apprehended swiftly by LA police.

33

The rain in Spain

It was a mighty sad day for both Gloria and I when our Pi contritely declared that the time had come for her to leave The House on Dundas and Vine.

Of course we had been fully aware for months that ultimately we would lose her, however, I guess to some extent we'd been in denial just the same. It was oftentimes so obvious from the blue in her eyes that missing her Mike was becoming insufferable to say the least. True, they managed to fit in long weekends together from time to time, but nothing compensated for the actuality of closeness and being together proper.

Pi had burned the midnight oil and deservedly been awarded her doctorate from McMasters and candidly there was scarcely work for her in Hamilton in any event.

And so, late into that Wednesday evening, saw the three of us briskly bundling Pi's baggage into our capacious Buick 8 Convertible for an early start Thursday morning, summertime breezy – yeah!

I recall that years ago our mother had referred to Mike as a 'slob'. Having said that I'll bet a dime to a dollar that Mike has been cleaning and polishing his fantabulous Brownstone since early this morning. It's not because of the effect that Pi has had upon him – withal they haven't shared a house together yet. It's overwhelming because the prepossessing sight of Pi gave Mike the need to become a better person than he thought he was. Pi realised that Mike's life was an unusual life and anything but tedious. Oftentimes he'd regale her with his salubriously generous interpretations of his adventurous escapades. For sure Mike's little lady would never be permitted to become bored – not in this life!

By all accounts Mike's agent Dora Pavel had gotten the lovebirds two return tickets to Almeria in Spain. Pan Am Flight 73 was departing JFK at 12 noon precisely the following day. Dora had organised a well salaried 4-week agreement for Mike working with director Jim O'Connolly. It's a sort of claptrap sci-fi Western called 'The Valley of Gwango'. Apparently the location of Almeria is substituting for New Mexico.

Mike's role was as a stand-in/stuntman for the lead star James Franciscus, who I'm told resembled each other. Dora referred to Mike's role as "small, but significant." She added "unlike your erstwhile UK movies, the director doesn't require you to disrobe!"

Mike almost forgot to mention to me that the buzz on the street said that James Franciscus was threatening to quit in the event that they didn't provide a stunt replacement for him. Inasmuch that the previous 'actor' lost his leg during a train chase scene!

Mike subsequently told me that the train scene wasn't so much of a problem as he had imagined, although he said that the crew were marginally skittish because of what had happened before. However, the covered wagon scene was filled with apprehension from the onset.

Pi was on the studio set every day, taking her own snapshots with this out of the ark Rolleiflex camera her grandma had given her years ago. Pi was immensely popular among the cast and crew and would howl with laughter when they oftentimes jibed "I would leave my wife for you Pi!"

Pi was cute. I think the fella's thought of her like a daughter and she was always gracious and always the lady too. Never what you call a tough broad like that Madonna is today, or indeed that Sinead O'Connor with a bald head who tore up the Pope's pictures.

Finally the day arrived when the wagon scene was scheduled. There had been a rainstorm, but the ground was still relatively dry and so the director decided to go ahead.

Another stunt man, Gene Hopper, and Mike were in a covered wagon supposedly skedaddling from a stampede and Indian attack. Mike said that, although he'd been given a crash course on how to control the reins/horses, there were six of them pulling the wagon galloping faster and faster! That said, Mike was clutching the reins as hard as he could, but had still inadvertently lost control.

Gene Hopper was just clinging onto the wagon frame like a tick on a dog and cursing a blue streak of obscenities from here to kingdom come.

In the future if any cinema aficionados who can read lips are watching they will be treated to their own personal choice of profanities, and then some! It's fair to say that we didn't have any actual prearranged dialogue – it was all ad-lib!

As they raced across the plain toward a ravine, Mike said he had sussed that they were in serious danger, inasmuch that they were headed toward a 30-foot drop from a volcanic escarpment which couldn't be seen on camera.

The wranglers could see it and wanted to intervene and stop the horses without delay, but the director refused to let them – until the very last second, and then it took six wranglers, with every ounce of force they could muster, to bring the whole shenanigans under control.

Before the wagon had come to a satisfactory halt Pi had raised her skirt above her knees and was running across the lot like all the demons in hell were chasing her. Mike and Gene had just instinctively clambered down from the wagon and were stood in the dust and dirt kind of traumatized. Mike said he recalled Gene's first spoken words "made it by a whisker Mike."

This wasn't a stand-offish situation for Pi. She threw herself around Mike with such intense emotional fervour that in doing so she practically caught all 6'3" of him downright off balance.

"Let's go back to Manhattan please Mike" she whispered breathlessly into his ear.

Mike undersold the recklessness of the director and just acted indifferent to what had happened by complacently commenting "It was way too close for comfort, but at least the director got what he wanted. After editing it will look really engaging on screen!"

Mike's take on the aftermath…

Back at the trailer that evening Pi had become a chatterbox personified. Australian beaches versus Spanish beaches – hemispheres and atmospheres; all sans souci stuff that proved beyond doubt that she had not recovered. It was as though she was intoxicated by the terror of the days events and how the outcome could have been so menacingly different.

"Come on, I'll wash that Spanish dust out of your hair for you." Pi enjoyed me washing her hair, but in the little bitty trailer basin it wasn't easy-peasy and soon soap and water were flying in all directions. I kissed her lustfully and got myself all soapy-eyed. She laughed what was an unpredictable laugh, and, like a backyard squirrel stealing my oranges, my zestful wife had re-emerged!

It seemed to me now that the 'Gwango' movie was quintessentially what I would refer to as a 'great-bad' movie. In other words, it became fun only because it was so utterly fatuous in nature.

Perhaps even the filmmakers themselves never actually realised that they were creating such trash. Perhaps they truly assumed that they were turning out what should have been a serious picture. At opening night when the audience laugh in all the wrong places the powers that be were going to be totally taken by surprise!

Despite all of that the movie was really entertaining, but only because it's so bad. You could sum it up by saying "It's impressive only in the extent of its awfulness."

I have a hunch that Pi might agree, however, when we fly Stateside in the morning I think the whole deal is best forgotten about!

34

Actors & spontaneity

I expect you've heard the aphorism that 'every story must have an ending'? It seems to me that it isn't always necessarily so.

For example, virtually all of the stories contained in these pages are anecdotes about real incidents and real people's lives. That being the case I am obliged to eventually draw my story to a close with a comma instead of a period; like Khrushchev and JFK! In any event I consider it somewhat disrespectful to end folks lives exclusively because the all-encompassing narrative dictates it should be so.

One thing that you can rely upon in real life is that there are no 'endings' per se – unless a person is pushing up daisies! Rarely does anything remain the same, or for that matter, how you might have envisaged it to be! Oftentimes the curve balls just keep on a-coming for no easily understood or explicit reason. Perhaps it's all just a part of our empirical evolution and nothing more besides?

And, therefore, dear reader, and explicitly to our Pi, who I shall attempt to broach later, thank you for coming to be part of our peachy family with all of its irregularities – we welcome you!

If I put on my thinking cap I recollect that our 'family' got under way during the early part of this decadent decade and now, ten years later as the 1970s approach, we have become somewhat scattered about. I cannot know what sort of breeze steers us unerringly toward unseen harbours, but I do know that the uniqueness of our extense – in all its forms – will bring us all together again, one fateful new day soon.

I sincerely trust that by welcoming my reader to our family I haven't kind of inadvertently betrayed the privacy of my other most dear compadres, inasmuch that their whereabouts is fairly privileged information. The fact is it may even enhance their popularity or notoriety and surely that isn't such a bad thing!

Before I shed light on all of that, I wanted to share with my reader a little bit about my characters that even they may find somewhat interesting:

In movies and stage plays, and indeed any forum where role-play is a prerequisite, it is the actors who are vital to success. Oftentimes it is feasible that the character the actor wishes to portray could fundamentally be a blurry extension of themselves. In which case an accomplished individual would almost undoubtedly be able to call upon their own emotional memory – an analogous emotion that they have used many times in their own lives.

This self-sufficient analogous energy is a factor that I have patiently endeavoured to capture in 'The House on Dundas and Vine.' Inasmuch that almost all of the characters contained in these pages authentically parallel their 'real' counterparts; we are left with entirely unelaborated and genuine folk telling the story as it is – who says reincarnation isn't possible!!

35

Vicky Vale

There had been a harsh reaction around town of late which had blown completely out of proportion. It was concerning Duffy's interminable run of new 'would-be' entertainers. The grapevine suggested that Duffy's dragon-lady and maitre d', Ernestine De Roche, was actually missing her fallacious face-offs with old contender Ricky Dale!

By all accounts Duffy's/Ernestine had kissed goodbye to a whole list of male and female vocalists who were ill-suited for Duffy's cloth cap regulars – several of whom indicated that they might take patronage elsewhere!

Truth be told, the old guard didn't cotton on to either contemporary music or indeed the fashionable new-fangled crowd it was drawing in.

However, in a Galaxy not too far away called Toronto, there existed a diner by the name of El Rancho on Queen Street, and a singing waitress by the name of Vicky Vale. I thought that maybe I had a responsibility to check her out and so, with that in mind and my Gloria in tow, we set out to investigate further!

We turned up at El Rancho just before 3pm and the staff were in the process of closing until the evening. It's curious how you can easily pick the head honcho out. They're the bod stood by the cash register adding up the takings!

"Sorry to interrupt you, I'm looking for a lady called Victoria Vane, I believe she works for you" I enquired.

"Oh Vicky" he replied. "She's at the hospital today."

"Is she sick?" Gloria asked anxiously.

He smiled. "She doubles as a nursing sister five mornings a week – are you friends of hers?"

I apologized for my tardiness and formally introduced us both.

"We were hoping to offer her a permanent role as associate singer with the Zito clubs and bars" I added.

The guy seemed to have Vicky Vane's schedule all lined up as he replied "She's singing 9.30-11pm at the Desiree Club on Queens tonight if you want to pop in and catch her act."

I thanked him and we returned to the car. Gloria looked at me kind of bemused – her comment paralleled my thoughts exactly. "Could be this gals got altogether enough on her plate without the Zito job as well."

I beamed ear to ear. "I concur my darling, but perhaps we should still get together for a talk and give her the once over!"

I knew the gaffer who ran 'Desiree' and so, with that in mind, we decided to be cheeky and knock-up the club before the punters began to arrive.

Vicky had just finished a run-through with the band which was the perfect opportunity to sock our proposal to her. Listening to her reprise with the band, her pitch sounded technically flawless; in fact she had a kind of emotional undertow that put me in mind of Sarah Vaughan.

After the mandatory shaking of hands we all found ourselves a private booth toward the rear of the club.

Gloria respectfully explained the whys and wherefores behind our unexpected visit and me, in an attempt to loosen things up, asked about Vicky's slick name and its similarity to my own!

"The heroine in the movie 'Now Voyager'" I inaccurately blurted out.

"No, sorry Ricky, she was called Charlotte Vale" Vicky responded and continuing she added "it was my mom who named me Vicky after the Gotham Gazette reporter Vicky Vale. Mom had a crush on Bruce Wayne – not so Batman though, he had Lois Lane in any event!"

Gloria cut in "Oh, Jerry, don't let's ask for the moon; we have the stars" and realising her error, she quickly came up with the correct answer "sorry; that was Victoria Vale!!"

Vicky was a truly personable lady – perhaps a nursing prerequisite – she thanked us and agreed wholeheartedly that a Zito family connection would distinguish her singing career, not to mention the financial benefit it would make to her purse!

After Vicky's final spot at Desiree, and when things had begun to quieten down for the evening, we all retired to the VIP Lounge to relax a while.

I mentioned to Vicky that my brother Mike was in the entertainment business and that he and his wife would be travelling up from NY to visit us at The House on Dundas and Vine on the forthcoming weekend.

Gloria chimed in cheerfully and asked whether we could persuade Vicky to join us. "It's only a small family soiree and you would be more than welcome to stop over afterwards – we do wish you would!"

It was at that point in the conversation that things began to take on a somewhat mystifying turn. Inasmuch that Vicky had no qualms at all regarding a stopover; the decision seemed to rest upon whether we were comfortable to have her 'special' friend tag along also?

There was a kind of 'pause' in the tete-a-tete. Not an uncomfortable pause, it was more 'involuntary', like we were 'out for the count'.

To her credit Vicky dived in first. "Sunnybrook Hospital on Bayview is where I work. It's not an ordinary type of hospital per se. Fact is it's a psychiatric institution. They used to refer to them as mental hospitals! For my friend to be able to socialize again, away from the confines of the institute, would be a mighty huge opportunity for him."

My Gloria was welling up and so I took the words out her mouth; definitively. "We would like to be part of this with you dear Vicky. If you feel you are able, fill us in about your mystic friend. You have the floor, now sock it to us – you needn't be alone!"

Vicky's relate:

"Sunnybrook was set up to cope with the enormous influx of Commonwealth POWs after their release and repatriation from North Vietnam. Folks assumed that only the United States were involved in the war, however, that wasn't necessarily true."

"We have pieced together that Eddie was shot down close to 10 years ago and was held captive in the notorious Hoa Lo Prison – nicknamed 'Hanoi Hilton'. He had suffered from some memory loss from the onset, but because he was an officer the North Vietnamese tortured him relentlessly, wrongly believing that he was withholding data and such. Eventually he escaped and in due course was found in a remote village near to where he was shot down."

"He's been with us about nine months and we've got some kind of rapport. For example, if I am off duty he demands to know when I am due back. The staff tell him and he forgets and asks all over again! Refers to me as his 'mate'."

Having composed herself Gloria turned to Vicky. "You tell your Eddie we are looking forward to making his acquaintance. If he's allowed to have an alcoholic tipple, ask him what he prefers? It's a good thing too that you spoke to us Vicky. Back in '64 Mike's wife Pi had just arrived in the United States from Australia. Her dad felt obliged to enlist in the war and was reported later as missing – killed in action."

"Pi took a while in coming to terms with losing her beloved Dad. Perhaps she may find some additional solace in sharing her pain with Eddie. Withal Pi's Dad and Eddie were both on the same page in that respect weren't they?"

36

Saturday!

I was looking forward to Saturday. I am sure we all were and when it ultimately came around everything we'd prepared for was going according to plan.

Mike and Pi had arrived early in the day on the enviable Vincent Black Shadow – both homogeneously suited and looking as leathery and cool as their especially unusual get-ups; they were the bee's knees and they confidently knew it!

I had become Gloria's 'suck-up' gofer and washer-upper in the kitchen, but satisfyingly got to sample her divine goodies – figuratively and literally!

Vicky and her beau showed up spot on time at 6pm. Seeing them together they really did look like a couple. She in her chicer than Greek blue two-piece and dapper Eddie wearing matching hat, jacket and trousers.

We got all of the friendly introductions over quickly as we could and, whilst Mike and Pi disappeared into the kitchen to make us coffee, Gloria and I showed our new guests around the House on Dundas and Vine.

Mike was wiping off the hapless dead insects from their helmets and flushing them down the basin.

"Does he resemble your dad at all Pi?" he asked.

"Not really" she replied. "My dad was more brawny, and poor Eddie is really quite skinny." She looked dead ahead as though she was giving the matter a second thought. "He does kind of conduct himself in the same manner as my dad would, but maybe that's because they are of similar ages?"

Mike took her in his big bear-hug arms and reasoned "I guess that underneath we were both trying to optimistically imagine that somehow Eddie could be a reincarnation – a sort of 'born again' dad, however, he seemed like a really likeable and good-natured fella and Vicky seems the type that will put him back together again.

Later into the evening when we were all sat around the dining room table complimenting our hostess on the scrumptious victuals she had treated us to, it seemed like the logical thing to hand out some small panatellas to our guests. All partook except for Eddie; said he had grown accustomed to being without smokes!

It was Pi who piped up suddenly. "Did you know that Joan Baez sometimes walks barefoot around New York City? When Mike was working one evening I walked down to Greenwich Village and there she was; wore a black cotton turtleneck, black tights and black flats."

Aware that this was a useless piece of information, Pi superseded with "What made you first want to become a nurse Vicky – seems to me it's more of a vocation than a career choice?"

Vicky smiled, like she was pleased that Pi had asked. "I was a GGC – Girl Guide Canada Senior section girl scout when I was 14 years of age and it was a prerequisite that I became a first-aider – I think I just liked collecting badges really!"

"Do you have Girl Guides in Australia Pi?"

"Yea we do Vicky, but the Abos catch 'em and eat 'em... sorry, that comment was meant to be funny, but it wasn't was it? Sort of thing my gramps would say."

"Yes, I was a very stringent Girl Guide too Vicky, from age five right up until dad and me relocated to the United States."

Pi pretty much had the whole group of us in her pocket now.

She wasn't what folks would describe as a 'lavish' conversation-alist, but once she started it was difficult not to be enthralled and engrossed by her Western Australian accent and the empha-sis given to every syllable.

Pi continued…

"Several weeks before Christmas we Guides were given the task of writing an Xmas poem – it was a competition of sorts. I was about six years of age and very reticent and shy. I really didn't relish getting involved in such things. However, my dad said that I should without doubt enter the contest.

"Dad and I often wrote scatty, weensy ditties together and to one another; that's why dad was convinced I stood a very good chance of success. And so, with my dad's belief propelling my pen, I set to writing a Christmas poesy, and blow me down when the troop mistress read out the results I had come second in the contest!"

"Well done our Pi!" Gloria was genuinely taken aback by Pi's account of what had happened. In hopeful anticipation she de-clared "Can you recall any portion of the composition Pi?"

"Yea I can. I remember it almost word for word, mostly be-cause when it was bedtime, after I'd had me piggyback upstairs, I'd almost demand that dad recite the poem to me. Listening to it had a wonderful soothing effect on me and oftentimes I would have fallen fast asleep before dad had recited the third verse."

With an ultra-affectionate frown across her cheerful face she perked "Would you all like to hear my rendition?"

The table almost literally became 'alight' – there were heart-ening yells of "go Pi go!" and such carrots of persuasion and then silence as Pi comported herself.

Like a maestro of mirth she stood up from her chair, curt-sied – systematically tapped the stem of her vino glass and in heartfelt earnest Pi began her 'soliloquy'…

"*Thoughts* by Pi Edwards Dale

Verse I
Cows have lovely thoughts
to keep
They saw Jesus fast
asleep
In the stable long
ago
This is a thing that all cows
know

Verse II
Horses stood around him
too
Eyes wide open all night
through
They saw baby Jesus
there
This is a thought all horses
share

Verse III —"

Pi unintentionally faltered; Eddie stared fixated into the wild exhausting despair in her eyes and she into the irrepressible pain in his. Their mouths blenching in a blue funk of panic. Dispensation from tribulation had made it by the endmost means it knew.

She could put herself to sleep now – noiselessly Eddie resurrected and recited the closing verse to his Pi:

"Shepherds found a lamb
to take
Lamb saw baby Jesus
wake
Lying on his bed of
hay
This is a thing lambs dream
today"

THE END

The House on Dundas and Vine

Where are they now – and what are they doing now – was there life after 'The House on Dundas and Vine'?

*Alas, regrettably (or not) time by its
very nature keeps passing;
represented through the same change as it did
13 billion years ago!*

Although in hindsight it becomes obvious that our splendid days of yore were almost bound to be numbered, I still nevertheless celebrate that we had them.

The light-hearted and light-headed laughter, our somewhat precocious behaviour, things that money cannot buy. They are still real to me. I feel them close by and I know they haven't really gone away – perhaps just taking a break!

Didn't we ever talk! Conceivably hundreds of sentences; taking care to not necessarily finish all we said. To set aside one iota for that rainy day.

It seems to me that the marvellous thing about having steadfast friends is <u>not</u> to feel obliged to finish all you say and to allow your intuition to recognise that rainy day when it arrives; as it has done now!

Vicky & Ethan

Vicky has the most beautiful smile. She definitely doesn't need a ton of goo on her face or unmoving lacquered hair to look every bit the star. When she graced the spotlight either at Duffy's or the many other more salubrious establishments in the city, the crowd adored her. Was it any wonder that by and by Vicky Vale was earning a lot more spondulicks than Ricky Dale ever did!

I found it somewhat curious though because Vicky never really expanded her repertoire of songs she liked to sing, at least not by very much. It was as though she had sussed what made her happy and what made her fans happy and she adhered to that formula. Her phenomenal success was undoubtedly down to 'repetition and rendition' and she sharp-wittedly knew it!

From time to time she introduced a new kind of burlesque style dancing into her act. It was slightly bawdy in nature, but it wasn't half bad and had a real allure among the older guys in the audience.

You have clearly guessed that it became impractical for Vicky to pursue her erstwhile 'Nightingale' profession. Ethan's (Eddie) convalescence and significant recuperation had given them both a new lease of life. After months of indecision they had finally found their idyll.

'Eddie' had slowly taken a backseat and Ethan had come into being again. "No more visits to the shrink" he says relieved. "We have a common saying back home (Australia) 'everything is Jake' or 'everything is Jakealoo.' Extended to Canadian it means everything is okay or fine and it is too!"

"I never ever imagined that one least expectant day I would not only have my treasured daughter reinstated in my life, but into the bargain I would become aware of falling in love with a person who is an authentic embodiment of everything I have sought after all of my life."

So said Ethan Edwards to Vicky Vale and less than 48 hours afterwards they were both married at Toronto City Hall's municipal office.

Pi, Mike, Gloria and I attended. Vicky's folks had been killed in an automobile accident by a traffic light jumper back in 1962, but Vicky managed to find out the whereabouts of her Uncle Joe and he attended at the last moment.

Joe was kind of 'rickety' and Ethan said that Joe imagined him (Ethan) as some kind of potentially crazed Vietnam veteran – the sort that makes you shudder when you oftentimes see them burning a Vietnamese village on CHML. Ethan decided to exacerbate Joe's flawed notion about what he (Ethan) did during the war. "Goin' to scrape all the loose paint off and repaint my trusty machine gun over the weekend" he piffled nonsensically!

Being as Ethan had been a POW, he had a disability compensation coming to him in due course – for his service-connected injuries. With that thought in mind and a rough idea of how much it was likely to be Vicky and Ethan were hell-bent on putting the money to some good use rather than see it frittered away.

Just several days ago they had put a deposit on the freehold interest of a newly built self-service laundromat on Burlingston Lakeshore Road.

They invited Pi to view the property with them. A thrill of excitement ran through her, especially the upstairs apartment which, apart from the usual bedrooms, had what the realtor called an 'unfinished bonus room'. Vicky was quick to suggest "that's for you and Mike when you stop over!"

It had a café latte machine downstairs in the shop too!

Gloria & Ricky

Yellow ochres, burnt oranges, bright reds, purplish mauves…
when autumn appears in the eastern townships of Quebec the
trees dress up in their blazing colours.

Gloria retired there last fall to be with her spinster sister.
They live in a high perched lodge at the top of a very steep dirt
road.

She is a volunteer school bus driver.

"Devon for me
That's where I'll be
Under the stars just like heaven –
One day I'll go back there I know
Back to my own lovely Devon"

Ricky retired about the same time as Gloria. He had suffered
from homesickness for years and consequently returned to his
beloved Devon.

Footnote:

Gloria and Ricky definitely intend to reunite some day soon.
However, they cannot yet decide on which side of the pond
they prefer!

Mike & Pi

"NY is in essence a space of beautiful contradictions and for that reason by verbatim it is homogenously singular and intensely unique"

– Ricky Dale

The Vale of Blackmore in Thomas Hardy's Wessex is close to being the self-same!

Contracts are by definition intended to be enforceable except when parties have agreed enough is enough. American Tobacco Company and Mike had agreed such!

When Mike and Pi chose to settle in the Dorset countryside and actively run an animal sanctuary the deal was clinched by a flea-bitten, skin and bone mutt they came across eating turds in Spain.

Who would have thought that a McMasters degree in Animal Behaviour would truly trump serving coffee on the Staten Island ferry!

At Bournemouth University they call him the 'Old Master' because 'pound for pound' Mike is martial arts mastermind. He coaches there three days a week.

Christina & Rocco

Other arms a-reach out to me
Other eyes smile tenderly –
Still, in peaceful dreams I see
the road leads back to you.
Just an old, sweet song
keeps Georgia on my mind –
Georgia on my mind!

After Megan and Paul had capped off their scholarships to some effect and were earning in earnest, Christina and Rocco decided on a change of scenery too.

For the two of them the North Georgia town of Blue Ridge was perfect! Situated deep in the heart of the Chattahoochee Forest it was idyllic and ideal for their beloved hiking. Rocco was able to keep a regular eye on his business operations in Southern Ontario through his intermediary and conciliare Paul who relocated to Toronto. And Christina, she runs a chic clothing and apparel boutique in downtown Blue Ridge.

For reasons not discovered or known about, Rocco has refrained from visiting Canada. His stock response is "I have no desire to do so!"

Megan & Paul

Megan works as a photographer for Vogue and Life magazines in the Big Apple. She is single, gay and purchased Mike's Brownstone from him last summer.

On photographing models she says *"I like them well-dressed in black high heels and not much else!"*

Paul is conciliare to the Zito Family. He is married and his wife is expecting their third baby in the spring. They have a somewhat luxurious art deco apartment above the old Royal Alexandra Theatre on King Street, West Toronto; an onyx marble bathroom suite too!

Asked about his work, Paul's stock reply is *"I am Godfathered and dumb – don't ask questions about my business!"*

And what of The House on Dundas and Vine?

(I said farewell before I returned to the UK)
In spite of all the riotous weeds, densely overgrown bracken and seemingly impenetrable pathways, The House on Dundas and Vine stands as upright and undaunted as it ever was.

Where sun filtered windows embellished its portals, now huge wooden panels of marine hardboard safeguard its exterior, each held steadfast with dowels and countersunk screws for perpetuity – or so it seems.

Myriads of momentous memories of Christmas trees and Christmas past, of silly misunderstandings and mistakes of no consequence and so-called disasters that didn't occur in any event. Now all holed-up behind concrete and brick. The wild virtuosity, the soft simplicity and the far-reaching fondness for one another that we came to know as love in The House on Dundas and Vine.

Though somewhat difficult for this writer to equate the reflections of that love somehow still reverberate through every creaking floorboard and every hidden nook and cranny. It is as though this happy, sad and yet serious house still refuses to be a mourner – it is cautious and patient and waits to be unlocked once again.

With one single sob I bid farewell; the wavelengths in my mind obsessing through every corridor and room. And yet, it took me all these years to realize that this house, our house, The House on Dundas and Vine was indeed the entity that held us all together and even now as it stands momentarily uninhabited, it will be victorious once again and again long after our calendrical decades are snuffed out – for what are we to it but mere mortals!

The House on Dundas and Vine

This was the instant, this was the place
Where love was born so unaware
Our course was set, ahead we faced
The journey that was ours to share

In memory of my baby brother Mike
July 21, 1951 – August 3, 2016

WHISTLING AWAY THE DARK

I often think this sad old world
is whistling in the dark
Just like a child, who late from school
walks bravely through the park
To keep their spirits soaring
and keep the night at bay
Never quite knowing, which way they are going
they sing the shadows away

I often think my poor frayed heart
has given up for good
And then I see a brave new face
in my neighborhood
So walk me home my darling
Tell me dreams come true
Whistling, whistling here in the dark
with you
Whistling, whistling here in the dark
with you.

Adapted from a Mancini/Mercer composition

The House on Dundas and Vine

SPOILERS!

Six instances among many where the author has combined fact with fiction:

QUERY : Did Ricky authentically marry Gloria?

REPLY : The character of Gloria was adopted from an actual person called Sherry. She is the bona fide daughter of Rocco Zito and was indeed married to Ricky.

QUERY : Did Pi and Mike watch the great Bobby Darin perform at NY's Copa?

REPLY : Not hardly – Darin wasn't performing at the Copa on that particular evening, however, Bobby Rydell was!

QUERY : Is there really a person called Christina who lives in Cornelia, Georgia?

REPLY : There most certainly is, but as far as I am aware she didn't wed Rocco Zito yet!

QUERY : 'The House on Dundas and Vine' – does it really exist?

REPLY : Unequivocally, yes it does! The author contemplated purchasing the property in the autumn of 2001. Having said that, it is located in the Erie area and not in Hamilton as referenced in the novel.

QUERY : Did singer Ricky Dale truly entertain at Duffy's Tavern in Hamilton, Ontario?

REPLY : Yes he did, but only on four occasions. He was primarily an in-house entertainer at the Brant Inn Club in Burlington, Ontario.

The House on Dundas and Vine

Also by Ricky Dale

Limberlost
A Semi-biographical account of famous soprano Krystyna
Comanescu, a virtuoso who has fallen from favour and seeks
to bring her austere demons to rest.

Limberlost II The Legacy
This book is the captivating sequel to *Limberlost*; in which
secrets galore are let slip and the truth is exquisitely
unearthed.

Limberlost III The Prequel
The prequel to *Limberlost*, and a most profoundly in-depth
telling of not only how it all began, but the why and the who
as well.

Cloudburst
An extremely personal insight into the fact-based account of
why lovers Dahlia Carriera and Sandra Comanescu choose
murder as a way of life.

I Knew The Bride When She Used To Rock 'n' Roll
A charming and emotional spooky tale, based on true
happenigs, which has been described as "Poltergeist meets
the The Sixth Sense".